Table of Con

A Ginny & Georgia Story

Author: Aaron Bailey

Chapter 1

Ginny and Georgia – A Ginny & Marcus story

If Ginny hadn't left her shirt on the change room bench...

Marcus and Ginny stood flush against the shower wall, listening intently. Max had just left, her footsteps faded away to nothing. But Georgia was still there, small s clothes announcing her presence. Ginny looked to her left at Marcus, who met her gaze evenly as he leaned against the wall, the need for silence holding onto them while they waited for Georgia to leave the change rooms.

As she stared into his serious eyes, it crossed Ginny's mind that they needn't really have kept silent when Georgia and Max had first entered and accidentally intrud intimate moment. But now their reveal would seem suspicious. So they kept silent anyway.

The moments ticked away slowly and Ginny began to falter under Marcus' gaze. His serious face was not something she could look at comfortably for too long, not quarters like this, not when moments ago he'd been about to kiss her. And she about to kiss him back. She glanced down at her hands, ears concentrating, but Geo moved yet.

Georgia made a small sigh from around the corner, and there was a fabric noise like the sound of sleeves being pushed up. And then the rustling of something else.

didn't dwell on it for too long, as Marcus had silently reached out a hand across her body and touched her waist. She naturally turned her body to face him directly.

already silent, wary of Georgia's judgement, his expression would have silenced her anyway. His eyes bored into hers; Ginny swallowed as an oddly pleasant plumm sensation gripped her. Marcus rubbed his thumb on her skin and he leaned a little closer, a lock of hair falling forward as he tilted his head towards her. Ginny glanc Georgia cleared her throat.

They both jerked their heads back, almost ricocheting off each other like bullets, and Marcus' hand was back by his own side in an instant. Ginny whipped her head Georgia was not actually looking down at Ginny like a bird of prey, talons extended ready to grab a small animal that dared leave its home. No, she was still around unaware her daughter was not out on the dance floor still. Georgia rustled a little more, and then her footsteps retreated from the room. Ginny held her breath as t quietened, and then finally released it as the door squeaked shut.

She turned back to face Marcus, and their eyes met again. Ginny felt her pulse in her head for a brief moment.

And then they connected.

He'd grabbed her almost roughly by the waist, and she'd grabbed his neck with both hands. They met in the middle, lips melding and hearts racing. He tasted like m smelled so familiar. He pushed her back against the wall, the cold tile sending a thrill up her spine. Ginny reached her arms up across his shoulders, and their torso together. So close together. Marcus found himself pressing his hips against her. He leaned down and grabbed Ginny by her thighs, lifting her suddenly. Ginny's legs around Marcus' waist naturally, and she gasped as she was pinned between the wall and Marcus.

Ginny lifted her head back. She needed a moment; her brain swirled and frenzied as she struggled to see through eyelids that wanted only to close and pull herself Marcus. Marcus stopped too, breathing through his open mouth, his eyes wild and fixated on her. Ginny became aware that she was trembling a little, as though ev body had come alive with sudden electricity.

'Um...' Ginny began, taking a forceful breath.

'Yeah,' Marcus said back. He trained his eyes back on her lips, and Ginny's stomach clenched excitedly.

Ginny kissed him again and Marcus returned eagerly, but then his earlier words popped back into her head. "I don't really do girlfriends", he'd said. And she remem humiliation following when first he'd clambered through her bedroom window, and the anger of the second. It didn't matter that her body felt on fire, that his lips ig passion, or that save for a few scraps of fabric he could be inside her again. The warmth from their surprisingly intimate conversation snapped away, and the affect vanished.

Ginny's brain was abruptly altogether cold.

She dropped her legs from around his waist and extricated herself awkwardly. She walked over to where she'd dropped her shirt in the shower. She'd been embarra she'd first walked in, taking off her shirt without a care, the blue material hiding Marcus' surprised form from her as she waltzed in and inadvertently performed a b uninspiring strip tease. She fetched it now from the floor, her cheeks flushed again with self-consciousness, and pulled it quickly over her head.

'Did...did I do something?' Marcus asked to her back, eyebrows drawn in confusion and rejection. She stood up straight and turned matter-of-factly to face him.

'You don't do girlfriends,' she reminded him, and his expression withdrew, leaving behind nothing but static. 'Plus, you're not-girlfriending with Padma. And I'm doin don't know what - with Hunter.'

They stared at one another in silence.

'So, I'm gonna go,' Ginny stated and she strode away from the showers.

She was halfway to the door.

'Wait,' Marcus said quietly.

She waited automatically. She cursed her legs, and inhaled a little dramatically.

'Yes?' He can talk to her back, Ginny thought with mild satisfaction.

'I don't do girlfriends,' he conceded, and she could hear him approaching behind her. 'But I don't have to keep hanging out with Padma.'

Ginny turned to face him.

'Why?' She looked at him intently, reading his expression. Confusion, hesitation, need...she saw these flit across his features.

'I...want to be able to hang out with you.'

'What, so we can have sex again? You're the one who asked me to keep it on the DL.' Ginny crossed her arms.

'I did, that's true,' he nodded, and his hands went to his pockets. Anxiety drew his shoulders up and he looked at her imploringly, his demeanour mirroring his first bedroom while he confessed his thoughts of her. In spite of herself, Ginny's emotional spikes softened. Just a smidge.

'What are you trying to say, Marcus?'

'I don't know. I'd just rather hang out with you than Padma.'

'Well, I'm not just going to be your sex friend,' said Ginny firmly. Not again. She held on again to her anger tightly, though Marcus' gentle expression loosened her

'That's not what I want,' Marcus said quietly. He looked down at his shoes now, taking a deep breath. 'I still think about you. I think I like you.' He looked back up a wide and vulnerable, searching her for requital.

'You barely know me,' countered Ginny, but her traitorous heart throbbed. Marcus stepped closer, looming over her.

'And yet,' he said, and he leaned down cautiously.

Ginny begged herself not to look at his lips, but the eyes weren't any easier. He waited for her, head bent, eyes locked on her, waiting for her to come back to him.

She did.

His kisses filled her with a sense of brightness and light in her heart, but heaviness and warm, rolling, pulsating thunder in her body. It was overwhelming.

She pulled back again, placing her hands on his shoulders to prevent him from leaning towards her again. She breathed hard.

'I kissed Hunter tonight,' she admitted, surprised when hurt jerked across Marcus' face. He recovered quickly.

'So don't kiss him again.'

'Are you going to kiss Padma again?'

'Not anymore.'

She believed him, she realised. Or hoped. His face held not a lick of jest. Ginny's arms dropped from his shoulders, and she crossed them.

'Okay, so...' Ginny wasn't sure where to go from here.

'So I won't see Padma...and you won't see Hunter...?' Marcus' cautious gaze met hers, eyebrows raised in question.

Ginny nodded shyly. Marcus smiled brightly at her. Excited nerves erupted in Ginny's stomach and she smiled back.

'I better get back,' Ginny said slowly, glancing reluctantly at the door. 'We were meant to be taking a photo...'

'Yeah.'

Marcus lifted his arm and saluted her, smiling conspiratorially. Ginny laughed and stepped back. Marcus began to retreat to the shower.

Longing rushed over Ginny, reached out to Marcus' hand and pulled him back. She kissed him briefly, firmly, intoxicatingly.

Ginny turned and left, eyes bright and face fevered.

The morning came, and Max effused her sadness over Riley. Ginny rubbed her back and shoulder.

'I'm really sorry,' Ginny said sadly.

They were interrupted by Press and Hunter.

'That didn't totally suck,' Press said. Ginny internally rolled her eyes at his tone.

'Are you kidding? That was lit. Best night ever,' Hunter grinned. He looked so bright and happy.

'Yeah! The best,' Maxine tried, but was clearly not enthused. Her eyes clapped on Hunter's hand. 'Is that a burrito? Yeah, I'll take it.'

Norah walked past then, supporting a visibly unstable Abby, her words slurred and playful.

'Whoa, Abby, are you okay?' Max walked after the awkward couple, taking her stolen delicious bounty and Press followed.

'That was for you,' Hunter said lightly, amused.

'She needed it more,' Ginny grinned.

'I had a good time tonight. I think you're awesome,' Hunter stated directly.

'Uh yeah, me too,' Ginny agreed. 'I mean you, not me,' she added after the fact.

They laughed a little, but Ginny felt discomfort rise up. Marcus came to her mind. She needed to end things with Hunter.

'Cool ... 'cause I wanted to ask you something.'

Ginny's stomach dropped. Oh no.

'You're smart, and obviously beautiful,' Hunter continued. Ginny's smile faded. '... And I was wondering if you wanna maybe...be my girlfriend?'

Ginny blinked. She took a deep breath. She wished her friends weren't only a few feet away, watching the drama unfold. Max was going to be so disappointed.

'Hunter,' she began, looking at him. His eyes changed immediately, recognising the apprehension in her voice, and Ginny stumbled. 'I-I like you, I do.'

Hunter pursed his lips slightly, waiting for the hammer to drop.

'I just...I think you're so nice, and you're obviously beautiful and smart too,' she took a shaky breath. 'But, uh, I don't really feel that way...about you...I'm sorry.'

It was then that a thrill of panic set in Ginny. Would MANG still want to be MANG if she made their group awkward by not being with Hunter? Would she cause a div being the newest addition naturally be sidled back on out? Would she lose Hunter as a friend altogether? She bit her lip and looked down.

'Uh...' Hunter started. She could see him put his hands in his pockets, and she looked back up to his face. She owed him that much. He was pulling his expression b but she read the rejection on it before it was gone. She looked at him sadly. 'That's okay...' he said finally. He attempted a winning smile, but it didn't quite reach hi

'I hope we can be friends though. But I understand if you don't want to...'

Hunter chuckled.

'Of course we can. I think you're great. Of course I want you as a friend.' He smiled at her, his eyes starting to shine. 'Uh, I'm gonna head off. I'll see you Monday.'

throat, and Ginny pretended she couldn't hear how his voice thickened, only nodding.

Ginny watched Hunter leave to the path on the right, and she caught Marcus watching her, leaning against a wooden post. So he'd caught the show. There was a sm lingering up-lift in his lips. Conscious of her friends having witnessed this all as well, Ginny looked away from Marcus' magnetic eyes and sat next to Max.

Max rounded on her, flabbergasted and temporarily distracted from her pain over Riley, her voice squeaky with surprise.

Ginny tried to shake her head clear and address Max's many questions. But her mind fogged with worry, and she ached to get home.

Ginny had kept up her end of the bargain, at great risk.

Would Marcus?

Chapter 2

MANG huddled together on Max's bed, drinking in the lewd sight on her computer.

Porn.

They giggled and squawked at the positions and expressions, tempted to withdraw but still not hiding their blushing eyes. All four faces contorted in various expres and consideration.

'That's a fun, new orifice,' Max remarked over the sounds of exaggerated moaning emanating from the screen.

'See? This is the problem with porn,' Ginny said confidently. 'It gives guys a messed-up view of sex and never prioritises female pleasure. That's why guys never ha what they're doing.'

The girls nodded contemplatively, while Ginny hoped she came across more knowledgeable than she felt. I mean, really, she'd kissed two boys and had sex once. H

on the matter.

'Ew, don't put it back there again!' Abby squealed, and they dissolved into laughter.

Norah's phone chimed.

'It's Brodie. He wants to know if we're going to the battle of the bands?'

'Oh, I'm so excited about that. Sophie's definitely gonna be there because her rock god friend Scott's performing. He won last year,' said Max.

'Padma joined 3SB now that Jordan left,' said Norah. 'She's meant to be pretty good.'

'Who is she again?' asked Abby. 'And do they have to change their name now?

'She and Marcus hang out,' Ginny said.

'It's gross,' Max nodded.

Ginny did not know if this was still true though. A few weeks since the Sophomore Sleepover had passed, and Marcus and Ginny hadn't really talked. Sure, she brie Max's house and she found herself looking out her window periodically. But she had been the one to end things with Hunter, and Marcus hadn't yet chosen to updat with Padma. As far as Ginny was concerned, he and Padma were still not-dating and that was none of her business.

It was his turn. She would not crawl to him.

'Do you think Hunter will be okay if I go?' asked Ginny.

'Please,' said Abby. 'Don't think too highly of yourself.' But she grinned at Ginny.

'He'll be fine,' said Max, pulling her into a hug. 'And if he's not, we can hide you in the back.'

'Gee, thanks.'

'You're welcome,' Norah said, deftly tapping a reply on her phone.

o

o - o

o - o - o

o - o

o

In her bedroom, Ginny thought about the battle of the bands. She hadn't spoken to Hunter since she declined to be his girlfriend. She'd made brief and uncomforta with him, but they currently had all the space they could possibly want from one another. She pulled out her phone to text him, anxiety rippling. Was this kind of co like Abby implied? They'd only gone on one date, two if you included Sophomore Sleepover. Hunter was over her by now...or even still in love with Sam according t Ginny took a deep breath and started typing.

G: Hey.

H: *Hi*

G: I just wanted to ask, are you

okay if I go to battle of the

bands?

H: Yeah. That's fine.

You should come

G: Okay. It'll be nice to see

you

She watched as Hunter began to type, and then stopped. She waited a little. But he didn't type again. Ginny sighed and strode over to her window for some air, sco Marcus' bedroom across the way. Hunter was a nice guy, and would have been a really nice boyfriend. He seemed to have really liked her. Ginny could have really l maybe one day.

But she gave that up. She'd picked passion again, like a fool.

Marcus strode into view across the way, pulling off a shirt and replacing it with a shirt for bed. He glanced out the window himself, caught her eye and nodded at he unfriendly. Ginny pulled a face and walked away. He was annoying. Her phone dinged.

M: Howdy, neighbour

G: Hello, Marcus

M: How's it going?

Ginny grimaced at her phone, and made her way to the bathroom. She started brushing her teeth.

G: Just dandy. You?

M: Okay.

We haven't talked...

G: No, we haven't

Marcus began typing, and then stopped.

Great, chasing them all away today, thought Ginny. She stared at her face, a familiar pinprick of discomfort in her eyes. She took a heaving breath, and exhaled slo little.

Had Marcus only wanted her for sex? But not so much that he was actually willing to stop seeing Padma?

Shame hit Ginny hard. Deep and burning in her throat and gut. It spiralled her mind. She pressed her left middle fingernail into the fleshy pad of her thumb, buryin as she could. She hurried out of the bathroom and back to her room, stewing. Tears free-fell before she could stop them and she doubled her efforts, digging into h as well. It hurt, but not enough. She looked at the lighter on her desk, gasping a little.

Her window slid open, and Marcus stumbled through. He smiled at her, then his face froze.

'Ginny?'

She backed away from him.

'Please leave,' she nodded at the window, sniffing and blinking away her tears. She tried to wipe her eyes surreptitiously. 'I'm not up for an impromptu visit today.'

voice down, remembering that Austin and Georgia were nearby in their own rooms.

He stared at her, taking in her red eyes and wet face.

'What's wrong?' He took an anxious step towards her.

'What part of 'please leave' don't you understand?' she spat.

17

He stopped, and held his palms up defensively. But he did not leave.

Ginny strode towards him angrily.

'I said get out.' She pushed his shoulders, steering him back to the window, ignoring his confused and hurt face. 'You don't want me, so I don't want you here. Go.

Padma, I'm sure you'll be very not-happy together.' Her voice choked up slightly.

Why did she pick him? Hunter had been right there, had asked her to be his girlfriend. And she hadn't spoken to Marcus in weeks, and now he's popping through he like a stray cat for a convenient meal.

'Padma?' he asked, bewildered. 'I ended things with Padma weeks ago.'

'Oh, really, then why haven't I heard from you?'

Marcus hesitated.

'I didn't...know what to do...'

'Well, here's what to do. You turn around and you climb back out through the window.'

'Ginny, I...' He started, as Ginny laid her hands on him again and tried to push. But he was ready this time and stood his ground. 'Don't push me, Ginny, please.' An arms around her.

Ginny seethed in his arms. But there was something about the way he held her and his presence. She felt that wall crumble a little; the one in place to keep her sa Marcus had his own damn personal hammer and chisel for it, apparently.

18

'What's wrong?' he tried again, murmuring into her curly hair. She felt him press a light kiss to her head and she started to quake with sobs. He tightened his arm a waist and pulled her a little closer, one hand going to the back of her head. She almost expected him to shh her like a little fussing baby, but he just held her. He pr her head again, this time for longer.

He waited patiently, not saying a word, while Ginny's tears ebbed after the initial explosion. She pulled back to look at him, eyes watery. He was calm and sincere, curls that clung to her face to the side. Ginny inhaled unevenly. She felt...safe. She felt wonderful?

'You don't have to say anything if you don't want,' he finally whispered, gently wiping a tear from her cheek.

'Marcus, why haven't you spoken to me? I was waiting to hear...'

'I actually thought you were avoiding me...but then I saw you through the window just now.'

'I wasn't avoiding you, I've been at your house multiple times a week!'

'I know. But you're always with the bro squad, so I stayed in my room.'

'They're my friends,' Ginny said defensively.

'I know.'

They gazed at each other for a moment.

'But you...you broke things off with Padma?'

'Right after Sophomore Sleepover.'

'Oh.'

Ginny leaned back into his hug, placing her head against his chest. He put his other arm back around her. They stood silently in her room for some time, pensive. H

chin on the top of her head.

'I've missed you,' he admitted.

Ginny felt a rush of affection. She and Marcus both moved to look at one another, and their lips met in a gentle, lingering kiss.

'I'm sorry I pushed you,' Ginny said when they pulled apart.

Marcus nodded and he leaned back against the window frame, and Ginny against her desk.

'I do want you,' Marcus said firmly.

'What?'

'You said I didn't want you. I do.'

'Oh.' She brushed a hand through her hair.

'So...are you okay? Do you want to talk about it?'

Ginny shook her head, and smiled a little, remembering the last time one of them was upset around the other.

'Maybe we just need to chill out,' she quoted, taking his hands in hers and lifting them up. 'Sorry, I don't have a shower in here.'

Marcus smiled, and kissed her with fervour, pulling her hands up further. He walked them towards the bed, and they fell heavily down on the mattress, kissing and Ginny reached under Marcus' shirt he suddenly pulled back, looking awkward.

'Um...'

Ginny sat up, and drew her knees to her chest.

'What's wrong?'

'Uh, when we last...hung out...' he looked at her significantly, 'did you finish?' He dropped eye contact towards the end and he fidgeted with her bedspread. 'I heard in Max's bedroom earlier...'

Ginny flushed.

'Not really, no.'

'I'm sorry,' Marcus said earnestly. 'I thought you did.' He looked a little bashful.

'It's okay. It's not your fault.'

Marcus pulled a face at her bedspread.

'No, seriously. I've...never had one before.'

He looked up at her then.

'What? Not even by yourself?'

Now Ginny pulled a face.

'Gross. No.'

'It's not gross,' he laughed a little. Ginny shushed him.

'Keep quiet. Mom and Austin are here.' She glanced nervously at her door, and jumped up to place a large bulky sweater across the foot of the door. When she turn Marcus was eyeing her from the edge of her bed in a way that dropped heat in her belly.

'Come here.' His voice was husky, and she did, swallowing. He pulled her to stand between his legs, placing his hands on her hips. He looked up at her, fingers touc of her pants, raising an eyebrow. She nodded at his questioning expression, and he stood up so that he could comfortably snake a hand under the material. Ginny's together as he touched her, unsure how to feel. 'Does that feel good? Be honest,' he murmured.

'Um, I think so.'

'Hang on.' His hand withdrew for a moment, and Ginny's eyes opened wide in shock to see him put two fingers in his mouth. The fingers he'd just had down her pa

'Gross!' she admonished him. But he shook his head.

'It's not gross.' His eyes darkened as he gazed at her.

And he put his hand back down. Ginny gasped, and blinked rapidly. Marcus smiled warmly at her expression.

He pulled her pants down slowly, turned her around, and led her to sit on his lap on her bed. She leaned back into his chest as his hand continued on its merry mis new. This was unexpected. This...this was what people were talking about, she realised. Marcus began to kiss the side of her neck, pulling her hair aside for access her ear made her shiver.

22

'Still okay?'

She nodded, and her breathing deepened, leaning into him. Marcus' spare hand urged her face to his, and they locked eyes. She should blush, she should avert her she fell deep in the dark pools of his expression. Marcus was reading her; he'd opened her like a book he'd read a thousand times but never this chapter. Ginny rec vulnerability she shared with him, her anxieties and her tears, her lust. But by gaining passion from him she was also giving him power. Power over her heart. Ginn more safe or more scared.

Chapter 3

Ginny had a text from Hunter.

H: Could I meet you at Blue Farm today?

Ginny chewed her lip as she pondered, and wiped the drowsiness from her eyes, head still firmly wedged in her pillow. What harm could it do? She'd be seeing him battle of the bands anyway. Maybe he wanted to break the ice before seeing each other in front of all their friends again outside of school. It was one thing to polite eye contact in class or as they stood by berry tree, it would be quite another at a social event.

Ginny thought of Marcus, who'd kissed her softly as he backed out her window last night, and saluted her from the ground with a wide smile. He didn't seem to car convention, so she wasn't concerned about him acting jealous and told Hunter when she was free. And then Max sent her 3 texts in a row about Sophie.

Ginny rushed over to the Bakers' house. It was a Sophiemergency. Apparently.

'Okay,' Max said, holding out a variety of shirts to Ginny. 'Which of these makes my boobs look best and is most likely to make Sophie look at them?' Her face was Ginny appraised the shirts and fixed Max with a stern eye.

'Max. You do not need to reveal yourself to make Sophie like you.'

'But I want her to see them and fall irrevocably in love with me. Boobs are the window to the soul, probably. I know I'm lovable, but why not put my best boob forw pulled up one shirt. 'This one is tight,

24

but not necessarily revealing. This one,' and she picked up another, 'has like a window...'

'Max, no, you are more than your boobs. Society has just made all women feel like our bodies are all we have to give.'

'Yeah, but that's patriarchy.'

'So?'

'So I'm gay, and the person I want does not have a patriarchal penis.' Max grinned devilishly.

Ginny pulled a face, while Max laughed indulgently.

'That may be so. But Sophie will like you for who you are. Just be yourself.'

Ginny pulled out a bright yellow shirt with a large open mouth.

'See, this shirt makes me think of you, it probably talks a lot,' Ginny laughed. Max feigned offence.

'Okay, but this shirt looks good on me. Good choice, Sophie will love it.' Max flounced over to start looking at pants. 'So, speaking of the patriarchy.'

'Mm?'

'Are you ready to talk about Hunter yet?' Max eyed Ginny from over her shoulder.

'Um.'

'Come on, I've waited weeks since you first blew me off about it. That's longer than I've waited for anything. I've been so patient. Please reward me. Answersssss.'

'There's not really anything to say,' Ginny fibbed.

'But why? Hunter is so hot and so nice. And you're so hot and so nice. You're the perfect couple.'

'I like him, I do. He's nice. He was really sweet on our date.'

'So, what happened?' Max paused and sat on her hanging chair, watching Ginny.

Ginny swallowed, searching for a reason that would appease Max. She was like a puppy, her eyes round and confused, waiting for the next treat. Ginny had met Ma first, that's what happened. The brother that Max kind of hated. The one that if Max knew how Ginny felt about him, she might never speak to her again.

'I guess I'm just not ready.' The lie fell out of her mouth before she'd thought it through.

Max's eyes lit up and she squealed.

'Oh, Ginny, you like him! Oh, that's so sweet, you're all nervous. Don't worry, just be yourself and it'll all be okay.' She paused. 'Huh, that's what you said about So smart. Ugh, and so is Sophie.' Her voice took on a plaintive quality as she pulled out her phone to look at Sophie's Instagram.

'Hey, loser.' Marcus had appeared in Max's doorway. He nodded at Ginny, no indication on his face about last night's events. He pointed at Max, and Ginny decidedly from his hand, having less of a poker

26

face than Marcus and strongly remembering how he had used that hand on her barely 10 hours ago. 'Where's Mom and Dad?

'They went to brunch, now leave,' said Max without looking up from her phone.

'Ah.' Marcus said, not looking particularly surprised, then looked at Ginny. He indicated his thumb over his shoulder and raised an eyebrow in question.

Ginny glanced at Max, who was still distracted by her phone, and shook her head at Marcus with wide eyes. Marcus silently brushed off her concerns, and jerked his the door.

'Ugh, Marcus, why are you still here?' and Max looked up at him in disdain.

'Just saying hi to Ginny,' and he backed out the doorway with a smile, and walked across to the bathroom on the other side of the hall.

Ginny longed to go after him.

'I actually need to go get ready for work,' Ginny brought up.

'Oh, good, I'll come with!' Max leaped to her feet and lead the way out the room. Ginny followed meekly, watching Max take off downstairs.

As Ginny walked past, Marcus came back out the bathroom, surprising her. She saw him see that Max was waltzing out of sight downstairs, leaving them alone. He opportunity and kissed Ginny, walking her backwards through his open bedroom door and up against his closet door. She gave in for a moment or two.

'Can I see you tonight?' he whispered, in between kisses.

27

'I''m going to the battle of the bands with MANG.'

'So cancel.'

And she was sorely tempted as he kissed her neck.

'I have to go,' Ginny said, both about the battle of the bands and his room, pulling herself out of Marcus' compelling grip. She paused at the doorway. 'But maybe a flitted downstairs after Max, with Marcus' grin consuming her mind.

o

o - o

o - o - o

o - o

o

Ginny had managed to send Max home from Blue Farm Cafe, having been followed the whole way to work and assisted on her shift while being kept up to date with thoughts on Sophie. Catastrophe struck when Ginny accidentally liked Sophie's Instagram photo from 2 years ago, and Max left as a cringing, stressing mess. Ginny in precisely five minutes. Hunter ended up arriving in four, being prompt as he was. He smiled at her as she wiped her last table.

'Hey, I'm off in just a sec. You can grab a seat.' Ginny indicated to a handful of clear tables, and strode back behind the counter, confirmed briefly with Joe that he h for her to do and removed her apron. Ginny took a moment to compose herself away from Hunter, but nevertheless some energetic butterflies rustled her nerves.

She sat across from Hunter, and smiled cautiously.

'Hi,' Hunter started. He looked nervous too, Ginny thought, and took some small comfort in that.

'Hey.' Ginny placed her elbows on the table, lightly crossing her forearms. She drew in a deep, anxious breath after a few moments of eye contact.

'So, I wanted to talk to you,' said Hunter. Ginny nodded. 'I know things have been kind of awkward these past couple of weeks...'

Ginny laughed in agreement, and Hunter joined in with good nature. It was almost an in-joke.

'I thought we should talk...I told you I wanted to be your friend, and I meant it, but if we're too awkward to even say anything around each other we're doomed. A here, and I don't want to make it any harder than it needs to be.'

The last part surprised Ginny by how considerate it was. He really was nice.

'Okay,' Ginny agreed. 'I wasn't trying to be awkward, I was just trying not to make you uncomfortable. I didn't want to do anything before you were ready.'

'I know,' Hunter smiled at her, and his expression grew oddly knowing. 'But, like our first date, I think we should skip over it and get juicy with it.'

Ginny laughed, but she felt a weight being lifted from her stomach. Maybe she wasn't going to inevitably lose her new friend group.

'You're really okay?' she asked. Hunter nodded, but his eyes held hers for slightly too long, and Ginny tried to work out the odd twist in his expression. Hunter put a Ginny's briefly, and her eyes widened in confusion.

'Yeah. So I'll see you at the battle of the bands, then?' He began to stand up. Ginny, a little shaken, followed suit and they walked out the door together.

' There you are,' said Georgia, who was just getting out of her car parked outside the care. 'Honey, come on, we have to go set up for the poker night. Hi, Hunter.' G

warmly at him, chivying Ginny over to the car.

'Bye, Hunter. I'll see you tonight.' Ginny buckled herself into the car. Hunter waved at her.

'Oh, are you guys going on another date?' asked Georgia playfully as she turned the engine over.

'No, Mom! It's battle of the bands and Hunter is playing.'

'Oh! Well break a leg, Hunter. I'm sure you'll drive the girls wild.'

' Mom! '

o

o - o

o - o - o

o - o

o

Marcus texted her late.

M: Look outside

Raising an eyebrow, Ginny went to her bedroom window and saw Marcus lingering cautiously in the front yard, seemingly trying to hide from view of the lower leve

'What are you doing?' she whispered. 'Just come on up.'

'No, you come down,' he said. Ginny looked at him incredulously.

'My Mom won't let me out this late.'

'I figured. To be clear, by 'come down', I mean 'climb down'.'

Ginny scoffed, peering directly down the window.

'No, thank you. I'm not Spider-Man.'

Marcus just smiled at her expectantly. Ginny eyed him critically.

'Fine. One sec.'

She ducked her head back inside, and quickly pulled on some sensible shoes suitable for last-minute wall-scaling. Ginny slowly and awkwardly climbed out her wind

'Good, now reach your leg out to the porch roof,' Marcus instructed from below. Ginny did so. 'And now you need to lower yourself down and put your foot on the fi ledge.'

Ginny tried, her fingers valiantly staying in place as her foot aimlessly reached for the ledge. But Ginny was much shorter than Marcus, something he did not appea accounted for, and her foot only touched air. Ginny wobbled in the air.

'Marcus,' she gasped, and her arms began to shake. 'Help.' She looked down. The ground wasn't that far away, but she was not looking forward to dropping onto it

'Oh, shit,' he said, rushing forward to grab Ginny around the waist. 'I've got you, let go.'

'Marcus, don't drop me.'

'I've got you.' He tightened his arm around her waist as he said it.

'I'm trusting you,' Ginny said severely. Marcus laughed, and he looked up at her from her midriff, but on seeing Ginny's serious face he quietened.

'Ginny, I've got you.'

They stared at each for a few moments, before Ginny's arms began to give way.

Ginny gingerly let go and her full weight fell onto Marcus, true to his word, who gripped her strongly around her waist and safely lowered her to the ground. He did and they breathed hard, falling into a kiss naturally. Aware that they were standing directly in front of the living room window, Ginny pushed them towards the mai took Ginny's hand and pulled her away and into the street.

They strode quietly for a number of minutes. Ginny's ears felt oddly hot as Marcus continued to hold her hand. He'd held more than this of her before, but this was intimate. Marcus led her to a nearby park filled with trees and shrubbery lit with twinkly lights, and winding walking paths.

'Is this where I see you sneaking off to at night?' asked Ginny. Marcus grinned.

'Sometimes.' He made a bee line for a particular bench and sat on it. 'It's peaceful here,' he said simply.

He pulled out a little baggie from his pocket, where Ginny spied several rolled joints.

'Do you mind?' he asked, joint already between his lips as he fished his lighter from another pocket.

'Not as long as you share,' Ginny said sleekly, sliding in next to him on the bench. Marcus smiled, lighting up and taking a deep drag and passing it to Ginny.

'Does this have any special instructions?' she asked blankly.

'What?'

'I've only done this once and that was with a bong, and there were very particular instructions.'

'Not really. Just inhale, hold for a bit, exhale.' He smiled at her, and a part of Ginny felt like it glowed.

Ginny didn't care for the taste of it too much, and it was hot. She coughed the first time. They shared it back and forth for a few minutes, and then Ginny's head be fuzzy.

'Oh,' she said. 'There it is again.'

She looked over at Marcus, whose eyes looked as glazed as hers felt. They said nothing, just looking at each other blearily and fondly as the sound of chirping insec up. Ginny looked around.

'Is this all you wanted to do?' she asked.

Marcus made a face of careful consideration.

'Yeah.'

Ginny laughed. Loudly and free. Marcus joined in with her after a few moments. Ginny felt like she could see her laughter; it spilled out of her mouth like wispy cott away on the night breeze light as a feather. She watched it go, an elastic and buoyant sensation building in her chest. Happiness. She looked at Marcus, his eyes, h stock of him, his expression and her response.

'You make me happy,' she said breathlessly.

Marcus smiled warmly, and he leaned in for a gentle, savoured kiss. Ginny realised her face and body felt soft like marshmallow, and when Marcus held her she mo touch. He put his forehead against hers, and she felt a distinct sensation of merging and oneness, and the tickle of his hair; she worried that it might hurt when he

'I really like you, Ginny,' he whispered.

They stayed with each other until Ginny felt her body return to normal, and it began to get too cold. The feeling of oneness remained post-high as they walked toge beyond when they parted after Marcus helped hoist Ginny back to her bedroom. As she crawled through her window Ginny began to wonder for a short time about like and love, and what it was that made up the distance between the two.

But Georgia was waiting for her, stern expression withering the last of the glow from Ginny.

'And where have you been, young lady?'

Chapter 4

Ginny crossed her arms defiantly for strength under the glowering eyebrows of her mother, who surveyed her like a hawk. Caught red-handed climbing back throug past midnight was not a good look. She stalled, taking off her shoes and hoping she was sober enough to appear steady.

'Virginia Miller, you tell me where you've been right now.'

'Out,' said Ginny.

'Well, yes, I saw that.' Georgia's voice was lilting, almost musical. 'When I saw you wiggling through your window I did assume that you had been outside. What I w know, my darling underage daughter, is where you were and who you were with.'

Ginny didn't see any scenario where she could tell Georgia who she'd been with, at least not without making everything worse.

'Why are you in my room?' Ginny deflected.

'You didn't say goodnight. I came in to check on you before I went to bed. Only to find your window open and you not here.'

Ginny fixed her mother with an obstinate, sour face.

'So you came into my room without permisslon.'

Georgia's eyebrows raised dangerously on her forehead.

'Don't even think about turning this around on me. You are 15 and I came into your room to find you missing. No sign of any struggle, so I assume you left volunta don't write, you don't call.' Georgia began to pace in font of Ginny, her hands gesturing emphatically. 'I'm okay with you doing a lot of things Ginny, but leaving the telling me where you're going is not one of them.'

Georgia squared off in front of Ginny.

'I'll ask you one last time, missy. Where were you, and who were you with? I won't ask what you were doing, because I can smell the pot on you from here.'

'I was with Max,' said Ginny. 'She found some of Marcus' stash hidden in her room. She thought it'd be fun to smoke it.'

'Her room?' Georgia said suspiciously, searching for holes in Ginny's story.

'No one checks Max's room,' Ginny supplied easily, stealing her words directly from Marcus. 'So he hides it there sometimes.'

Georgia eyed her beadily, her eyes sweeping across Ginny, unconvinced.

'Hmm,' Georgia said. 'Well, I'll deal with you in the morning since you're back in one piece, and it's so late. You're a very bad daughter for making me miss some be She pulled Ginny in for a hug. When she pulled back, Ginny saw a poisonously polite expression on her face. Georgia walked innocently towards the door, shutting o

'Tell Max I just love her perfume. Mm, so masculine. Night, peach.'

Ginny closed the door behind Georgia and flopped face-first in defeat on her bed for several shameful minutes.

Her phone dinged in her pocket. Ginny reached down awkwardly and brought it up.

M: Goodnight

And he sent her a selfie, hair tousled, face relaxed. Ginny felt a pang of wanting. She took and sent a photo too, curls everywhere, eyes soft and smile gentle.

Ding.

Another selfie. This time he was clearly lying in bed and had removed his shirt. His eyes were dark and moody, cheekbones stark.

Ginny's heart throbbed distinctly. Nervously, she pulled her own shirt off and took another photo in kind, exhilaration pounding in her ears and sharpening her brea nose had been astute; Ginny could smell Marcus' cologne as well, or whatever he wore – removing her shirt had whipped the scent up around her, and her mind flo Marcus. His presence lingered with her, the silk of his lips and the weight of his gaze settled heavily in her stomach and lungs, anchoring her to the earth. He'd plan her, growing and twisting his way like ivy across a house. As Marcus sent her another photo, Ginny reached for earphones and got under the covers, removing her underwear. With a trembling finger, she initiated a voice call.

He said her name, and Ginny felt a hook pull her navel, dragging her down somewhere warm, comfortable and sensuous. All this time Marcus had snatched away h sensations he brought leaving her buffeted and billowed in his wake. But this, as she explored her own body for the first time, was something else. This, as she hea same, gave her fever and chills, gave her strength. She revelled in being forthcoming, high on the autonomy of wanting, taking, and having. It turned out sex can g passion and power.

o

o - o

o - o - o

o - o

o

Ginny stared at her pill. Georgia had pulled her out of school the very next day after Ginny's late-night return, marched her into the doctor's office, and signed her monthly subscription. The anti-baby kind.

'Since you're off cavorting with boys and lying to me about it, I at least want you prepared,' she'd said. Then she'd glared at her. 'Have you had sex yet?'

'No,' Ginny had lied.

'Well, wait a couple of weeks to make sure the pill is working. And take it every day at the same time.'

'I know, I was there in the doctor's office. I heard the instructions.'

'Well, good, at least you're listening to somebody. But please. Please tell me before you do.'

And that had been it. No grounding, just medication. No 3rd degree to confirm her company on that night. Ginny was surprised, especially as she'd thought that Ge just start sniffing the boys Ginny hung around, seeking a matching scent.

Those requisite couple of weeks had passed since being put on the pill, and Ginny was at Norah's with the rest of MANG, getting ready for Brodie's Halloween party hiding in the bathroom, thinking of

39

Marcus as she took her pill at 7pm like clockwork. Their first experience together had been, not a disaster, but she knew it hadn Ginny wasn't sure if she was ready for a second. Ginny's first instinct was to confide in Max. But she couldn't. If Max knew she was on the pill, she'd ask why. Ginny explode. But she took her pill, and buried the blister pack at the bottom of her bag, shuffling back to Norah's room.

Ginny was ready to let loose a little, and dance and drink her stress away. As the 'Baby One More Time' Britney, Ginny felt she clearly had the supreme costume. Sh little pink pom-poms in her wig.

'Max, you look amazing,' said Abby, as Maxine made some final wig adjustments.

'I knowww. Thank you,' Max simpered. 'Red jumpsuit is one of Britney's best looks.

'Do I look okay?' Abby asked, her hands pulling at the pants she wore.

'You look hot, like Madonna's gonna come here just to make out with you. Or I will if Madonna doesn't show.' Max grinned flirtatiously at Abby, wiggling her shoulde Abby looked pleased, and fixed the angle of her hat.

'Norah, that legit suits you,' Ginny offered, as Norah finished sweeping her blonde wig into a neat bun, locking her Toxic flight attendant costume in place. 'Jordan's it.'

'I might have given him a little preview after I bought it,' she smirked.

'You blew our reveal?' Max gasped. 'What utter betrayal.'

'Don't worry, I swore him to secrecy. Or he won't get into the mile high club with me.' Norah said it so casually as she applied some mascara that they almost didn'

they shrieked and laughed. Norah grinned.

Max gasped.

'Sophie just texted, she's going to be late. What do you think that means? Is she blowing me off?'

'Yes,' said Abby.

'No. It means she's late,' Ginny said sternly. 'Relax, please. You've been stressing out about this way too much. Now let's go.'

They paused in the mirror briefly, 4 stages of Britney Spears. Ginny felt aglow and wholesome. Ginny felt connected. As MANG pulled sexy faces in the mirror, she w the girls. She wasn't the 'other'. She smiled brightly, and began to push Max forward.

'Come on, let's go!'

Brodie's party was already in full swing as they arrived. Norah texted Jordan to get a Britney song put over the speakers, and Max made her grand descent down th went last, channelling the pop icon to the best of her ability. She danced, and smiled. She laughed. She was happy.

It wasn't until Bracia arrived and failed to hide her judgement of Ginny's costume that Ginny was reminded. Right. She's black. And she's white. She's neither.

The world suddenly shifted. Her costume was no longer comfortable. Her friends became aliens and the people responsible for perverting her identity, somehow ma white while also fist-bumping her and pulling her into dance circles to twerk. She'd even worn that basic white girl sweater and infinity scarf earlier. Had she forgott erased a part of herself? Had she fetishised herself?

Ginny escaped to the bathroom, greeting Abby briefly as she did so. She wanted to vomit. Pangs of grief and isolation lurched her stomach. The blonde-haired wom mirror revolted her. She hated her. Ginny watched her breath rise and fall, and hated it. Anger seeped in her veins like poison. She wanted it to stop. She needed it sheer force of the pain threatening to overwhelm her. She wished for her lighter, and noticed a lit candle on the vanity. Ginny stretched out her arm.

She reached the sensitive flesh of her wrist over the tiny flame, and measuredly brought it down until it seared her skin. It worked like magic, sapping all her pain f to her arm. She held still until she began to shake, and all she could feel was the need to save herself from the fire. Reset, Ginny could face herself again. It wasn't She wiped her tears gently, steadied her breath, and went back to the party.

Hunter approached her comically, his vampire cape held across his face mysteriously.

'I vant to suck your blood,' he said dramatically in an impression of Dracula, but coming off very much like The Count from Sesame Street. 'But I am a friendly vam haff to suck this jello shot instead.' He offered her a small cup with bright green jello, and cheers'd her. Ginny downed the shot with Hunter and tried to smile at him smile faltered.

'Um,' Ginny said, fishing for something to say.

'Are you okay?' He dropped the accent, and she could see him looking critically at her. Could he see the redness of her eyes?

42

'Yeah, I'm fine,' she grinned. Hunter looked unconvinced. He put his caped arm around her shoulder and led her back upstairs to a quiet room away from the bathr by the posters of women on the wall, Ginny assumed this was Brodie's room.

'What's wrong?' Hunter sat on the unmade bed and looked at her sympathetically.

'Nothing,' Ginny said, unconsciously trying to tuck her hair behind her ear, and foolishly flipping back her blonde pigtail in the process. She bit her lip as she felt a t discomfort in her stomach. She leaned back against a desk and looked at her shoes.

'You don't like your costume?'

'No. Yes.' Ginny paused. '...I don't know.'

'Is this about Bracia? I overheard you two...'

Ginny gazed at Hunter. She measured the shape of his eyes and the features of his face, the colour of his skin.

'I just...I was reminded that my identity changes depending on who's looking at me.' Her eyes dared him to laugh at her struggle, to invalidate, to make light. She unleash, wound tight like a metal coil, at the slightest hint.

But he nodded.

'Yeah. I'm half Taiwanese, half Caucasian, so I get it. It sucks. Hard.'

Ginny breathed.

'Yeah!'

43

Hunter smiled gently in understanding.

'I'm sorry you're having a hard night.' He stood up and walked over. He pulled her into a gentle hug.

Ginny was surprised, but hesitantly returned it. She remembered the awkward hug from their date; this one compared favourably. Hunter's arms tightened around slightly. She didn't mind. Ginny smiled sadly in solace; this was something Hunter was uniquely able to empathise about amongst her friends. As Ginny leaned her Hunter's collar, a remarkable sensation of closeness enveloped her. He was warm, and he was nice.

Ginny remembered Marcus.

'I better get back...' she said softly, and relinquished Hunter. He nodded awkwardly. They walked back in silence, glancing at each other briefly.

They didn't speak again at the party, and Ginny left in a hurry after Max dissolved into a weeping mess following a disastrous interaction with Sophie. She struggled to her home quietly, the alcohol making her both easily-distracted and a little stubborn. Marcus saved the day when he arrived in Max's room, and he wrangled Max into bed without alerting Ellen to their plight.

Ginny and Marcus lingered together outside Max's bedroom, eyes deep and gazing.

'Marcus,' Max's voice came from behind her bedroom door.

Marcus glanced at the door, but largely ignored her. He checked over Ginny's shoulder, then leaned in for a kiss. A familiar swooping sensation lifted Ginny's spirits.

right.

'MARCUS!' Max would not be denied.

Marcus pulled back and rolled his eyes.

'Meet me in my bedroom?' he whispered, not letting Ginny look away.

Ginny nodded, and made a show of walking downstairs.

'Bye Ellen, bye Clint!' She signed goodbye over in their direction, having been taught by Max. Once outside, she crept over to the trellis underneath Marcus' bedroo felt a brief worry about what might happen if the neighbours saw her, but climbed up anyway.

Marcus' room was different than she'd expected. There was a beautiful eye painted on the wall, lovely colours overlapping. Ginny was staring at it when Marcus wal didn't turn to face him. She was surprised to feel tears start to brim.

'What do you see, Marcus?' she said quietly. Her voice was low and unemotional.

Marcus walked over to her, clearly confused by her sudden change of mood. She could see him follow her gaze and glance at the eye on the wall.

'What do I see...?' He was looking at her, searching for more information.

'When you look at me. What...what do you see?'

She didn't know what she wanted him to say. She swallowed nervously, and tipped her head back to prevent the tears from falling, lips quivering. Marcus fidgeted o brushed a hand through his hair. Ginny took a moment in the silence to pull off her blonde wig with disdain, throwing it on the floor at her feet. She released her ha bun, tipping her head forward to loosen it and flipping her head back. She felt bare. Nude. Revealed. She pressed a finger to the burn mark on her wrist, clenching Marcus put a hand on Ginny's back and searched her face for an answer or a cure to her pain.

'Ginny, what...?'

Ginny turned to face him, and the tears spilled over, but she waited for him to answer. Marcus was visibly confused and pained.

'I just...' He struggled to put his thoughts into words, so unprepared for this level of questioning. 'I just see your eyes.'

He fixed her with such a look that it halted her tears. She read the meaning on his face through the hair fallen across his features, even if he hadn't uttered the wo if he never would. She reached for him, pulling him back to her as the truth struck Ginny in her navel and chest.

Marcus Baker saw her.

Marcus Baker loved her.

Chapter 5

Ginny climbed carefully out of Marcus' window, pausing as the white shirt of her Britney Spears costume got caught on the interior side of the frame. As she freed it, she looked back at Marcus who gazed thoughtfully at her from his seat on his bed.

'Good night,' she whispered, eyes bright and breath thin. Her heart was still pounding from a feverish kissing session that Ginny had not wanted to end. She'd pulle bed, skin flushed and lips parted, suddenly ready again and over-willing to have Marcus inside her. She'd pushed away her horrid thoughts of race and identity, pref delight in the feeling of wrapping her legs around Marcus' hips and bringing him closer, abruptly aware of how intimate her skirt allowed them to be. They had given moments of keen movement and longing, hands gently brushing over skin and mouths uttering gasped desires. But he had eventually pulled away, murmuring abo to check in on Max.

He responded to her whisper from the window with a mildly ironic salute. He may have been trying to look unbothered, but Ginny's eyes lingered on the way his to with more heave than usual and the frustration knitting his eyebrows together.

Ginny smiled brightly at him.

'Soon,' she promised, and started backing down the trellis.

Marcus rushed over to the window and stole another kiss from her, hands pulling at the back of her neck.

'Don't do that,' Ginny said, inhaling wistfully.

Marcus frowned in concern.

'It makes it harder to leave. And also I really don't want to fall.'

Marcus' eyes softened, and she resented him just a little bit for the knots it gave her stomach.

'So don't leave. Stay tonight. It won't take long to check on Max.'

'We made a mess of things enough the first time. Frankly, I'm glad you brought up Max because I was...' she raised her eyebrows and exhaled sharply, '...complete again. But I don't want your mind to be anywhere else. And I probably shouldn't have been crying literally five minutes before.'

Marcus nodded.

'I also would really like you to not immediately leave the bed,' Ginny deadpanned, eyes daggered. Marcus had the good sense to be abashed.

'Yeah,' he agreed. 'Those are all fair points. The first time kinda sucked, didn't it.' He watched her reaction.

Ginny considered her words.

'Sucked is not the word I would have used.'

Marcus looked at her expectantly.

'Misguided?' Ginny offered politely.

'Tragic?' Marcus countered, eyebrows furrowed in seriousness, but his tone was playful.

'A Series of Unfortunate Events?'

Marcus laughed at that one.

'Borderline problematic because you climbed through my window without permission?' Ginny continued. 'Which, by the way, can you message me before you do tha

"I'm about to enter your home and don't know how to use doors" text would be appreciated.'

Marcus pulled a guilty face, looking to the side.

'Yeah, sorry about that.'

'All three times?' Ginny prompted.

'Yes. Sorry. You're right. It is very, very weird that I came through your window.' He paused. 'Was it...just a little bit romantic and sexy though?'

'Not at all,' Ginny said firmly. 'And you should not take the fact that I had sex with you as an indication that it was. In fact, that definitely happened in spite of your climbing. Please text me if you feel the overwhelming desire to scale my house from now on.'

Marcus nodded, looking contrite, and murmured sorry at the window sill. Ginny watched him measuredly, and gave him a firm kiss, and felt a surge of pride as she ignite in his eyes.

'You're forgiven.'

They kissed goodbye and Ginny climbed away before her body convinced her to stay.

'Ginny,' Marcus whisper-yelled when she reached the ground and threw her blonde wig down. She caught it, gave Marcus one of his own signature salutes and walk house. At least she had a positive memory coming out from this costume now. She mentally tightened the lid on the thoughts of crisis that Marcus had been able to away. Without that feeling that Marcus gave her, that sensation that he saw her in a way no one else did, those thoughts grew stronger in her mind and gnawed at

o

o - o

o - o - o

o - o

o

Wig in hand, Ginny walked through her front door.

'Ginny, you're here,' said Georgia, seated on the armchair uncomfortably with Austin beside her on the ottoman. There were two people on the couch. Ginny couldn from the backs of their heads. She walked further in, and recognised with confusion and surprise the lady with long, stringy blonde hair that she'd degraded as tras small kid that she had served at Blue Farm not too long ago. Having never expected to see them ever again in her life, let alone in her house, Ginny was stumped a

'Hi?' she said uncertainly.

Georgia sighed.

'Meet your cousin Caleb and your aunt Maddie.' She said it with hesitation and resentment.

'Hi, Virginia,' said aunt Maddie, while cousin Caleb smiled at Ginny.

Ginny took a brief moment.

'No,' she said. 'Nope, I'm not doing this.' And she walked swiftly out the room.

Georgia sighed.

She sighed? Georgia just dropped a giant bomb on Ginny, and she's sighing?

Very suddenly, Ginny decided – actually, she would do this – and marched right back in there, anger boiling over.

'You said – you said you didn't have any family. You said your parents were dead, you said it was just the three of us!' She stared at Georgia in accusation.

'Hm. Our parents are not dead,' said Maddie awkwardly, sucking in air through her teeth. There was a pause of silence. 'Well, we'll give y'all a minute.' She rose up heading out the room. 'Caleb?' Ginny's new cousin followed her new aunt.

'What, and I cannot stress this enough, the absolute -'

'I'm sorry, okay?' Georgia interrupted, standing up. 'I should have told you,'

'You think? Why are they here?' Ginny spat.

'I don't know. I haven't seen my sister in over a decade. They're gonna stay tonight and we're gonna figure it out tomorrow.'

'They're gonna stay here with us?' Ginny stared at her mother in complete disbelief.

'I like them,' Austin piped up.

'Shut up, Austin!'

Ginny knew he was too small to understand the severity of what was happening. To Austin, he had just gained two family members. To Ginny, she had just lost her

'Hey!' Georgia reprimanded. 'That's not how you talk to your brother.'

'Yeah? How am I supposed to talk to my brother? Do I not speak about him for 15 years and pretend he doesn't exist?'

'Ginny!'

But Ginny was too angry. She couldn't feel bad about yelling at Austin, and she wasn't paying attention to the lines of worry etched on her mother's face. Maybe it w day with an identity crisis, or perhaps the fact that her mother had lied to her for 15 years was simply enough, but Ginny's fury swept across her like lava. She wish wearing this stupid costume, and felt humiliated to be having this particular conversation dressed as a pop idol.

'You know what?' Ginny threw the wig in her hand on the ground. 'I was an idiot 'cause I believed you when you said this place was different. But I shouldn't believ comes out of your mouth. God, who are you?'

'I am still your mom.'

'Are you? Because my mom is an only child. You – you're some weird, secret-keeping trash. You can't just lie to me, to us! It's not enough that you move us from t town. Now we've got secret family members?'

Georgia's face was one of shock, as Ginny's tirade kept going. She couldn't stop, the hate and vitriol flowed freely.

'How am I supposed to live with you? How am I meant to talk to you? How am I supposed to trust you? You just lie, and you move, and lie and move and we're jus following you. Don't you care what that does to us?'

Georgia made to open her mouth, but Ginny let out a guttural scream of frustration and stomped to the front door.

'Where are you going?' Georgia yelled.

'Anywhere but fucking here,' Ginny muttered, and she slammed the door behind her as hard as she could. She wouldn't stay in that house tonight if you paid her. T

With that random woman and her kid? With a mom she suddenly couldn't trust? No way. Not when she had another option.

She was storming across the road and halfway up the trellis to Marcus' room before she remembered their conversation from before. She held awkwardly to the wa her phone from her skirt pocket, typing a quick one-handed message.

G: Can I come back over?

M: Sure. I'm still up

It wouldn't do if Ginny had told Marcus off for climbing through people's windows without permission if she turned around and did the same barely ten minutes late the climb to his window and knocked on the glass quietly.

A bemused Marcus opened it a few moments later.

'Um, how fast do you move? Because I only just got your text.'

He helped pull her in. As Ginny's feet landed on solid ground, the shock of the argument with her mother began to fade and it revealed the pit of sadness and betra There are some things that you should just be able to count on, Ginny thought, and your mother's family situation as she'd advised it to you was one of them. Wha lied about? Her whole life suddenly looked made up, fabricated by the whims of her mother and whatever details she chose to embellish or omit.

Ginny took off her shoes and her Britney socks and cardigan. She slid without a word into Marcus' bed and let out a forceful sigh. She rolled onto her side and looke glumly. The confusion worn on his face didn't stop him from sliding into bed next to her. He pulled her close, and Ginny was too sad to enjoy the swoop in her belly his arm around her side.

'What's wrong?' he whispered.

'I just...I needed something...stable,' she said finally.

'And you picked me?' he joked.

'I picked this feeling.'

She placed a hand on his forearm and squeezed, arching her body into his. She latched onto that spark that existed between the two of them, she focused on it, dr bit of light and breathed it into her lungs.

Behind her, Marcus' breath hitched and he leaned forward to kiss her neck in response.

Ginny knew she couldn't get carried away. Marcus was growing distracted from her obvious distress, and she had to admit she was too. But she wouldn't let their se sullied by her mom's revelation.

'Can I stay here tonight? I just can't be in that house.'

'Yeah.'

He didn't ask any more questions, which Ginny appreciated. They lapsed into comfortable silence, one of Marcus' thumbs stroking her stomach. The rhythm of his t her thoughts, and she sank deeply into the security of his touch, the roar of her worries quieting. Marcus placed a kiss on the side of her head, warmth blossoming point he touched. Slowly, she fell asleep, the cares drifting away and all replaced with comfort and closeness until she had the strength to deal with them tomorrow o

0 - o

0 - o - o

0 - o

o

'Marcus! What? Wh- what is happening? Oh my god, get up! I can't believe you! What is wrong with you? Who is that?'

Ginny woke abruptly to the shocked yells of Ellen.

Oh.

Oh, no.

Ginny had not thought this through.

Ginny was on her side facing Marcus, face nuzzled into his chest, one of his arms still wrapped protectively across her. Ginny looked up at him – he was also turned towards her, hair flopped all over his features. Apparently he was a heavy sleeper, he hadn't stirred at all.

'Ginny?' Ellen continued, and the bed covers were ripped back abruptly, shocking Ginny's system with cool air. Ellen strode around the other side of the bed and gla from over Marcus' back.

'Um.'

Marcus groaned, looking over his shoulder at Ellen blearily, and pulled Ginny in more tightly. Ellen's narrowed eyes latched onto him. Ginny's eyes went wide – wha her next steps here?

'Mom, it's too early.'

'Oh, it is not too early for the absolute pain I am going to rain down on you, Marcus. You are grounded, you are punished. You – are in so – much – trouble!'

'Mom, Ginny had a hard night, please.'

Ellen glanced at Ginny. She seemed to notice that they were fully clothed, and the wind flew out of her sails. Just a little. Ellen went over and closed Marcus' bedroo stormed back over and stared at them. Okay, plenty of wind in those sails still.

'You two have five minutes to give me even one explanation.'

Marcus looked down at Ginny. Ginny awkwardly sat up, allowing Marcus' arm to fall to his side. Ginny was suddenly very conscious of the fact that she hadn't brush last night.

'Can I go to the bathroom?' she asked, feeling like she was in school. 'Could I borrow a toothbrush?'

Ellen stared at her.

'There's a pack under the sink.'

Ginny shuffled off Marcus' bed and ducked quickly into the bathroom. She glanced at Max's door – still shut. Good.

After brushing her teeth and wiping her face with water, Ginny went back. Marcus had sat up and was gazing disinterestedly at his legs while Ellen paced.

'Okay, Ginny. What's happening?' Ellen put her hands on her hips.

Ginny blushed. She hadn't even told Marcus, and now she was telling his mom.

'Something weird happened last night when I went home,' she started.

Ellen raised an eyebrow, and Marcus looked up at her.

'Uh, I found out that my mom has been lying to me my whole life. She's always said she didn't have any siblings and that her parents were dead.'

Ellen and Marcus shared similar faces of surprise at where the conversation was going.

'I walked in the door last night,' Ginny's voice began to rise as the anger bubbled up again at the sheer audacity of her mother, 'and found out that I actually have a cousin, and mom's parents aren't dead, and my aunt and cousin are here? And they're apparently staying in our house? And Mom just wanted me to be fine with th doesn't throw my entire life, my entire existence into question.' Ginny's rant ended with a choked sob.

Ellen did not seem to know what to do with that.

'I didn't feel comfortable anymore,' Ginny continued, placing one hand on her opposite elbow, looking at the ground. 'I'd just been here, so I came back.'

'Okay,' said Ellen with consideration. 'But why are you in Marcus' bed? Why not Max's? And why were you cuddling?'

Ginny wasn't ready to provide an answer. What good reason was there in Ellen's mind to sleep in her teenage son's room? She glanced at Marcus, who met her gaz concern. What possible explanation was there for finding them so close, even if they managed to explain her presence in his bed?

Looking back at Ellen, Ginny realised she didn't really need to answer. The knowledge was there in Ellen's face, she was just waiting for them to admit it, like a ches planned 16 moves ahead to lure you into checkmate. Ginny looked back at Marcus.

'Uh...'

'We're sort of...seeing each other,' Marcus finally murmured.

Ellen raised her hands to the sky in frustration.

'And you think it's appropriate to be sharing a bed, do you? You're fifteen, Marcus!'

'We didn't do anything!' he defended hotly.

'That's true,' Ginny said. 'I promise, we didn't have sex. I was upset, we just cuddled.'

Ellen flicked her eyes between the two of them, seeking out any hint of mistruth.

'And have you had sex at all?'

Marcus pulled a face of disgust.

'Ugh, Mom.'

'Oh ho mister. If you're old enough to have girls in your bed, you're old enough to hear your mom say the word sex. Sex. Sex, sex, sex!' She aggressively signed se and Ginny's eyes widened at the display. ' How long has this been going on?' She indicated an accusatory finger between them.

'Since around battle of the bands,' Ginny said quietly.

'And you haven't had sex?' Ellen asked again.

'No,' Ginny said.

It was technically true. They had indeed not had sex since battle of the bands. Marcus gave Ginny a side glance, and hid his smile.

Ellen leaned away from them, and exhaled greatly. Her shoulders finally relaxed, and it looked like the storm was over.

'Well, Ginny, if you're okay now I think you should head home and talk to your mom. You won't find any of the answers to your questions in my son's bed.'

Ah, the mom tone-of-dismissal.

Ginny stood awkwardly and picked up her clothes, haphazardly pulling on her shoes. She and Marcus shared only a look of goodbye as Ginny backed out of the roo anything more. Ginny saw that Max's door was still shut, and then bolted.

Ellen was right, Ginny did want answers. Ginny's eyes narrowed as she looked across the road at her front door. She was sure as hell going to get them.

Chapter 6

Georgia was like a steel trap. Nothing was getting out of her. Ginny had pried and wheedled after she came from the Bakers' house. She'd yelled and stormed. She'd hurled insults and said things she didn't necessarily mean. But Georgia didn't budge, and come Monday Ginny knew as much about her m family as she did on the night of the party.

'We're not done talking about this,' Ginny had threatened as she left for school at the start of the day, ignoring her aunt Maddie and cousin Caleb who stood awkwa kitchen.

'Do you promise?' Georgia had muttered sarcastically.

The giant stone had dropped on them just as Ginny was starting to feel comfortable in this town. She had friends. She'd settled in and decorated. She had a, well, but she had a Marcus. She was this close to that perfect, ideal life. And now Georgia-being-Georgia threatened it all. Why couldn't her mom just be normal?

'Uh,' Ginny started. They were trying to be friends, so yes. But also, she wanted to go home and grill Georgia.

'Yes!' yelled Max, much too loudly for someone standing right next to them. She looked at Ginny with wide eyes and nodded at her encouragingly. Hunter's eyebrow little at Max's enthusiasm.

Ginny looked at Max, and a seed of doubt planted in her belly. Oh, no. Not overly pushy Max.

Marcus walked past at that point, and Ginny couldn't help but look at him. She swallowed nervously.

She needed all of Max's approval she could get. Ginny smiled at Hunter.

'Yeah, that sounds fun. Do we go straight there?'

'I can take you in my car,' Hunter beamed, and he held out his hand, indicating that he wanted to hold Ginny's backpack for her.

'Ginny!'

Frowning, Ginny looked over Hunter's shoulder at her mom, who was waving impatiently in the car park. She didn't normally pick her up.

'What?'

'We gotta go. Now.'

Ginny eyed her mom's clothes. Normal. Certainly not picking-up-and-moving-to-a-new-city clothes.

'I'm sorry, Hunter,' Ginny said apologetically. Hunter shrugged.

'Well, hey, we're thinking about doing some more practice on Saturday morning, if you want.'

'I think I can do that.' She smiled at Hunter and Max, and waved goodbye.

As she by-passed Hunter and walked towards her mom, Ginny saw Marcus leaning against a pole looking at her in confusion. He glanced at Hunter behind her, and His expression transformed into one of hurt, and he pushed off from the pole aggressively and stalked away from her. Ginny's heart plunged. She looked back over was engaged in a conversation with Hunter. There was no way Ginny could quickly catch up to Marcus without tipping off Max.

Inhaling sharply, she walked over to Georgia, pulling her phone out and typing an urgent text.

G: That wasn't a date invite.

'Come on, Peach, I know you're angry at me, but get your butt in the car,' Georgia chastised, climbing in the car quickly.

'Why, do you need to introduce me to my twin sister that I was separated from at birth or something?' Ginny shoved her phone away and got in the car with as mu one can muster for such a mundane act.

'No, I have to meet with Austin's principal.'

'What? Why?'

'He stabbed a kid in the hand.'

'What?'

o

o - o

o - o - o

o - o

o

Ginny seethed. Georgia had her metaphorical broom out and was continuing to sweep things under the rug. The secret family. Austin stabbing someone in the hand Like John Wick.

She wanted to scream.

Ginny's brain was struggling to process; there were things that just weren't adding up. Georgia loved her and Austin. She knew this. But Austin had just exhibited s exceptionally violent behaviour for someone his age – and she refused to take him to therapy, for reasons that Ginny was pretty sure had more to do with Georgia These two facts seemed at odds with one another.

Georgia had also lied about something critical – her family. For an important reason she had said, but now Ginny didn't know what was true and Georgia wasn't will anything further. What else had Georgia lied about?

Ginny felt words like selfish and immature floating around her mind as she pondered her mother.

She checked her phone again.

Still no response from Marcus.

Marcus was the only one who knew. Except for Ellen. And Ginny didn't feel like confiding in Ellen any further.

She could tell Max? Maybe. But Max was sad about Sophie and reluctant to talk about much else.

Abby?

She imagined how direct and flippant Abby's response might be. No.

Norah?

No, not even gentle Norah.

Dad?

She sighed, not ready to share with any of those options yet, and dared to double text Marcus.

G: Hey, we okay? I promise it wasn't a date.

Ginny went over to her bedroom window and looked over to Marcus'. It was dark over there. She looked back at her phone.

No response.

Ginny took a deep breath as the icy sensation of loneliness and isolation trickled down her scalp and into her belly. She glanced in habit over at her lighter, and dug into her palm. She felt very alone.

She threw her phone on her bed and sat at her desk, pulling out a textbook, thinking of doing some study. The booked leered mockingly at her, as if it knew that ev mustered the effort to open it, she wouldn't retain a single word. Ginny's eyes were drawn back to her lighter, feeling that overwhelming buzzing anxiety in her gut lungs and pricking her eyes.

She lurched upwards and rushed over to her phone, arms starting to tingle. Please.

Still no message.

Ginny gasped as the tears started, almost spontaneously, her lungs fighting against the stress holding them down. She turned and reached for her lighter, walking o against her door, locking out any potential intruder.

She pulled down her pants and held the flame to her burn mark, clenching her teeth as it scorched and healed her. She waited until a scream almost burst from her

Relief flooded over her, draping Ginny heavily. She was suddenly so tired. Life can just be...tiring.

Ginny hid her lighter back in its little pot and re-fastened her pants. She looked at her phone again – still no message – but she was too tired for it to really get to h Ginny crawled into bed and fell gratefully into sleep.

o

o - o

o - o - o

o - o

o

Ginny was surprised when Abby had given Ginny the chance to confide in her. Abby was brusque, but she also had a knack for getting straight to the point. And now an opportunity to her on a silver platter.

Austin had a therapy appointment with one Dr. Darmody tomorrow. With the one minor speed bump that Georgia would have to give consent due to his age. After Farm where Abby had apprised her of the appointment, Ginny had texted Abby to confirm the time and the phone number for the office, saying she would try get G

around and cancel the appointment if not.

Ginny took a deep breath. If Georgia could lie, so could she.

She hit dial.

'Wellsbury Therapy, this is Stacy. How can I help you?'

Ginny summoned her best impression of her mother. It might not fool someone from Alabama, but she thought it might trick the average Wellsbury inhabitant.

'Hi there, my name is Georgia Miller, my son Austin has an appointment with Dr. Darmody tomorrow afternoon. I was just wondering, you see I work in the mayor's had an engagement for that pop up tomorrow and I'm no longer going to be able to make it to take him there. I was just wondering, is it okay if my daughter drop checks him in?'

The friendly receptionist asked Ginny some questions to confirm her identification. Ginny was prepared, she'd written out Austin's date of birth and social security, a details to have handy in case they needed them.

'Okay, so that seems fine. The only thing is that we would need you to sign a document consenting to Austin's appointment tomorrow, just

68

as he's under twelve yea a best email address I can send that to you? You'll need to sign it and send it back, and all will be fine.'

Ginny balked. She didn't have access to her mom's email. She recovered quickly.

'Yes, that's not a problem. It's gmiller '

'Perfect! I'll send that off to you in the next couple of minutes. Just make sure it's sent back to the original address before the appointment tomorrow.'

'Thanks so much, you're a doll.' Ginny hung up, wincing. Was that too much?

Ginny pulled up her inbox, and grinned as the email rolled in. She was suddenly very thankful that her nickname coincided with her mother's initials. Ginny printed anxiously biting at her nails. She signed it with a flourish, took a photo and sent it back.

Part one of the great therapy caper was done.

Hunter had been enlisted for part two; he had agreed to pick up Ginny and Austin in his car and take them there.

Ginny clicked on her messages, and re-read Marcus' last one for the tenth time.

G: That wasn't a date invite.

G: Hey, we okay? I promise it wasn't a date.

M: Okay

Ginny didn't know enough about Marcus' texting to know if that was an okay-okay, or a that's-definitely-not-okay okay. She bit her bottom lip, and then her eyes w sent a text. She raced downstairs, yelling for Georgia.

'Mom! Max says our garden's on fire!'

'A fire?' came Georgia's voice from the kitchen.

They ran as one outside.

'My garden!'

'It's on fire,' Max pointed out helpfully from behind the safety of the garden fence.

'What the hell happened?' Georgia ran to the hose.

'Austin!' Ginny said, seeing him and Caleb running around

'Hey, you stop right there!' Georgia called out, starting to spray down the flames.

'Mom, the kid's starting fires! I know a therapist he can go to,' Ginny tried. Surely this, surely flames ten feet from her house would make her see reason. Maybe sh need to sneak him to therapy at all.

'What? No!'

Flames put out, Georgia moved on to scolding the kids.

Ginny scoffed, in complete disbelief. Georgia was being selfish, and Ginny filled with anger. She turned to Max.

"Can I go to your house?'

70

The girls crossed over the road and hid in Max's bedroom. Ginny sent off a message to her dad.

G: I miss you

After discussing Sophie once again, Ginny excused herself to go to the bathroom, closing Max's door behind her. She looked over at Marcus' door – open. She peere empty.

She sighed and decided she may as well actually go to the bathroom. As she came back out, Marcus was just coming back up the stairs.

He paused when he saw Ginny. He looked away uncomfortably.

Ginny glanced at Max's door, and pulled Marcus away from it.

'I don't like Hunter,' she whispered. 'It wasn't a date, he was just asking if I wanted to watch his band practice.'

Marcus stared at her as if she were stupid.

'And why do you think he did that?' he whispered back.

Ginny frowned reproachfully.

'Because we're trying to be friends.'

'Friends? He wants his friend to sit and watch him and his band muck around? That's a bad friend. Or it's a guy who wants his cute friend to watch him strut around

'Okay, so just to be clear, if Hunter is trying to make a move on me, you're getting mad at me, not Hunter?'

'You're the one accepting that ponytail's moves.'

71

'I was going to go as a friend.'

'Well, maybe I'll hang out with my friend Padma.'

Ginny blinked, and physically blanched away from him, as if she needed to see him from further back to take in the audacity.

'See?' Marcus said, his eyes boring into hers uncomfortably.

Ginny was hearing hurt and rejection. But all she felt from Marcus was anger and barbs.

'You're the one that doesn't do girlfriends. So let's just assume that Hunter does still like me, but maybe if I had a boyfriend he wouldn't have asked me. Did you th Ginny stared back at him, and Marcus looked away.

'You'd have to tell your friends.' He said it off-hand, to his shoulder. He hid his voice as much as he could, but he couldn't hide it from Ginny. She heard the note of sadness.

He looked back at Ginny, and she was surprised to see tears welling in his eyes.

'You think I haven't noticed?' he said, gesturing at Max's door. Ginny turned to look, still closed. 'You want me, you want to be with me, but not as much as you wa with the bro squad. So what if I don't do girlfriends? You aren't willing to even be seen with me in case it messes up MANG.' He practically spat the word at her.

Ginny took a step back, looking down at her wrists. His words shot through her like an arrow. She recognised the truth of it, and thought of how desperate she was how she'd agreed to go on a first date with Hunter at her keen insistence. She remembered watching Marcus' angry and hurt form retreating at school, not going a because Max might see. Hidden kisses in Marcus' room, whispers in the halls, charged eye contact as they passed at school.

Ginny swallowed.

He was right.

She looked up at him. Her heart ached. He seemed small and withdrawn; she saw him wounded and needing, damaged from hiding themselves in the shadows of G

loved her; Ginny knew it once more as he wiped his eyes and gazed at the floor. And she had returned that by placing him tidily in a cupboard, only to take him out convenient.

Ginny had been selfish. Ginny had been like her mother, placing her own comfort above the feelings and well-being of those she loved.

Ginny placed a gentle hand on Marcus' face, and lifted his eyes to hers. He was so vulnerable. She held Marcus Baker in the palm of her hand, an honour and a priv hadn't appreciated. She leaned up to him, reading the permission in his eyes, and kissed him so gently. He brought their foreheads together when they parted.

Ginny trembled as she steeled herself, inhaling his scent. She conjured him up in her mind, an amalgamation of the feeling of his smile, the comfort of his arms, th touch, the safety of his presence and the easing of her mind. She took a shuddering breath.

'I'm sorry,' she whispered. 'I love you.'

Marcus drew back suddenly to look at her, and she saw it again – he loved her. He took a deliberate breath. And then another.

Ginny couldn't resist, she leaned in for another kiss and stole the words away. His lips may have not have made the sounds just yet, but they imprinted the meanin and on her skin as he kissed her cheek and jaw.

He tried again when they pulled back.

'I love you,' he said, quiet and intense.

They smiled shyly at one another. Ginny squeezed his hand as a goodbye and walked back to Max's room.

She had a very short to-do list.

Tell Max about her and Marcus.

Get Austin to therapy.

Chapter 7

'Max?' Ginny said, gently opening Max's bedroom door and walking in uncertainly.

Her legs had turned to jelly on the very short trip from the hallway back to the bedroom, and her insides shook in fear.

Max looked up from her phone, meeting Ginny's eyes, looking concerned over Ginny's expression and tone.

'I...' Ginny started. She took a deep breath, and fixed Max with a serious face, feeling like she stood on the edge of a cliff. Behind her, land and safety – a world whe best and most delightful friend. In front of her, a place where she and Marcus are publicly together, where Max may no longer associate with her.

'What?' said Max, getting up and walking over to Ginny. 'What happened, you've been gone like two minutes. Did your whole house catch fire this time?'

'Um,' Ginny tried, twisting her fingers together. She walked away from Max and began to pace. 'Sit,' Ginny ordered.

Max sat, her eyes rapt on Ginny's journey back and forth in front of the bed.

'I have to tell you something,' Ginny said, briefly catching Max's eye before she looked away, away from those soulful brown eyes that met hers so innocently.

'Okay...' Max adopted an unusually serious face.

'It's about Hunter. Kind of.'

'Oooh, intrigue. I love secrets. Tell me.'

'No, this isn't intrigue. This is serious, and I'm really scared to tell you.'

Ginny's heart pounded in her chest, tattooing anxiety onto her ribs. She didn't know how to approach the topic. Chronological order? Most up to date information fi out a long breath, pausing in place and squaring off in front of Max. She opened her mouth. She sighed and started pacing again, wringing her hands.

'Oh my god, Ginny, just tell me. It can't be that bad.'

'I like Marcus,' Ginny blurted out – far, far too loudly. Her eyebrows rose up and she slapped a hand over her lips.

Max's eyes grew as large as saucers and her mouth fell open.

'You what?' Max rose up to tower over Ginny, her shock and incredulity making Ginny feel much smaller. Ginny cringed away from her.

'I like Marcus. I liked him since I came to town, and that's why I couldn't go out with Hunter.'

'You like Marcus? But he's an asshole! You like Marcus – my brother – th- that Marcus –' she gestured wildly in the direction of Marcus' bedroom, '– more than Hunte thought you said you liked Hunter, but you just weren't ready to go out with him?'

Ginny put her hands over her eyes.

'I lied. I just said that because I couldn't tell you about Marcus and I thought you would hate me if you knew, and I thought I might ruin our friendship if I said I did that way...'

'Oh my god, Ginny. I told Hunter what you told me and I told him not to give up. You've made me a bad cupid.'

'I'm sorry!'

'You're gonna have to break up with him again.'

'Again? We never got together!'

'You know what I mean,' Max dismissed.

'I'm not done, there's more,' Ginny said.

Max flopped on her bed, her hair spreading out as she stared in defeat at her ceiling.

'More? What could there possibly be? You like that floppy-haired stoner weirdo, I don't understand you, Hunter is right there, and you want my – ' she paused to fe my brother?'

Ginny went and laid down next to Max and joined her staring upwards. This was easier, no eye contact. She took a deep, clarifying breath.

'When I first moved to town...Marcus and I...kind of kissed.'

'What?' Max shot up to a seated position and stared at Ginny. 'When?'

'The first time I came over to your house.'

Max's eyes bugged a little out of her head.

'When I went to get a soda?'

'No!' Ginny defended. 'It was when I left...he was out with his motorbike and I took it for a ride.'

'You what?'

'I can ride motorbikes. That doesn't matter. Anyway, I took it for a ride down the street and when I got off the bike, he was just so cute and I was so attracted to h kissed him – I didn't even really realise I'd done it – but apparently I had.'

' You kissed him?' Max gaped like a fish.

Ginny continued on like a steamroller, all of the things she'd wanted to tell Max and held in with baited breath and fear. The words tumbled out of her mouth, and s poison of secrecy siphon away.

'And then after my date with Hunter, he randomly climbed through my window. And then we kissed again and then we had sex, and it was awful – the aftermath, th left and told me to keep it a secret – the sex itself I think was okay, but definitely could be better, but I don't know because we've only done it the once and I was a time.'

Max's mouth dropped open even further.

'And for a little I kind of hated him, I was so angry at him, ugh! And he tried to make a move on me after I told him I'd had to take the Plan B pill, but despite that into one another, and then we hung out at the Sophomore Sleepover and we actually had a really nice talk and we really connected and he shared things with me –

so close to him – and then he agreed to stop seeing Padma and I agreed to stop seeing Hunter.'

Ginny sat up again and looked Max earnestly in the eyes, who blinked at her in disbelief.

'And all this time we've kind of been keeping it a secret because I know you and Marcus don't really get along, and I just love you so much as my friend and I was t you would hate me for liking your brother and keeping it a secret, but I love you so much and I wanted to be your friend more – you're my best friend – and I'm so

– but Marcus and I have gotten really close and...and we kind of...' Ginny started to lose steam, as she took in Max's face that didn't seem to be comprehending any told her. 'I...I'm in love with Marcus, and I don't want to keep the secret from you anymore, you deserve to know and Marcus deserves to not be a secret.'

Max stared at Ginny.

'...and that's it,' Ginny finished lamely.

There were a few beats of silence.

'Hey uh loser. Dad said Mom's working late so we're on our own for dinner.'

Marcus had strolled in through the open door casually, clicking his fingers at the end of the sentence.

He took in Max's flabbergasted appearance and Ginny's stressed face.

'You guys okay?'

'I just told her...' said Ginny.

Marcus looked at Max.

'Ah.'

'I've never seen her this quiet before.'

'Loser, you okay?' Marcus waved his hand in front of her face.

Max blinked a few times, looking a little like a re-booting robot. She stood up and crossed over to Marcus.

'You climbed through her window? What are you, psycho? I hope you don't crawl through anybody else's window, you stalker.'

Marcus sighed.

'And you KEPT THIS FROM ME?' She folded her arms over her chest. 'Your twin sister? We shared a womb, we were womb-mates, and you just don't share this deta She rounded on Ginny, ignoring Marcus' disgusted expression at 'womb-mates'. 'And you! You're my best friend and you don't even tell me when you lose your virg lie to me about seeing my brother?'

'I'm sorry, I'm so sorry,' said Ginny. 'I didn't really mean to keep it from you, it's just that it first happened when we'd only known each other a couple of days and anything...' she glanced up at Marcus, 'and now it's definitely something.'

He gave her a small, sweet smile.

'Ew, don't smile at her, ughhh.' Max gagged. 'I don't know if I can handle this. I can't look at your face, Marcus, go away.' She put her hand up at him and swatted rolled his eyes, but waited for a nod from Ginny before he left. Then she turned to Ginny. 'I think I can still look at yours.'

'Are...are you mad?' Ginny asked quietly, looking at her feet.

'Yes. No. Kind of? I don't know! You said a lot back there, Ginny – love that for you, by the way, you should speak more – but it was a lot and I was not expecting i more revulsion, than anything,' she mused, her

80

voice turning contemplative. 'Like a deep, visceral rejection of the idea of my best friend having sex with my – hurk brother.'

Ginny dared to hope a little – tentative fluttering tendrils gripping her nerves.

'...I'm still your friend?' Ginny asked.

'Look, jury's still out...but yes. You have terrible taste in men – but yes.'

Ginny took a deep breath, and burst suddenly into tears, putting her face in her hands.

'I was so worried, and everything is so messed up right now with my mom and everything, and I haven't even gotten to tell you about that yet!'

Max looked sadly at Ginny, and pulled her into a comforting hug with a sigh.

'Sorry I've been so obsessed with Sophie. What else is going on, you weirdo? Is this about that biddy from Blue Farm? She was like a human Fyre Festival.'

Ginny wiped her tears, and managed a laugh, pulling back from the hug, so relieved to still have Max on her side.

'You can't tell Abby or Norah.'

'Ooh. It's gonna be good, isn't? I love sentences that start with 'don't tell Abby or Norah'.'

And Ginny regaled Max with the full tale, her heart lighter than it had been in days. Marcus came back in when it seemed calm, waving a white cloth of surrender.

'Ugh, fine,' Max said. 'Just don't kiss in front of me – or I will kill myself.'

When Georgia called and Ginny had to go back home to watch Austin and Caleb, Max and Marcus came with her. Playing The Floor is Lava, laughing and smiling, Gi moment of being genuinely carefree. She counted her gifts – her kid brother, her best friend and her – boyfriend? Lover? They hadn't really discussed it yet. Her Ma And then, as Georgia came home with a drunken sister and flirtatious moments with Joe, she counted her curses – her mother.

o

o - o

o - o - o

o - o

o

Ginny knocked on Austin's door.

'Come in,' he said quietly.

Ginny walked in, and saw Austin wipe a tear surreptitiously. Ginny sat on the bed next to him.

'Feeling any better?'

'No. I didn't want Caleb to leave. Or aunt Maddie. And Mom's all mad. I don't like it when she's mad.'

'I know.' Ginny put an arm around Austin's shoulder. He rested his head against her.

'Can we go on vacation again?'

Ginny looked over at Austin's books.

'Is later tonight okay?'

'Okay,' Austin said, sniffing.

Ginny took a steadying breath. She didn't have long to get her plan in motion.

'You remember when Mom had that meeting with your principal? And they mentioned that therapy might be something good for you?' She started casually, off-han Just a little subterfuge.

'Yeah?'

'I booked you a therapy appointment...it's today, in about forty minutes. One of my friends is coming to pick us up soon and take us there.'

'But Mom said she wasn't worried and didn't want me to go. And I don't want to go either.'

'I know,' Ginny said in a non-confrontational tone. 'Are you worried at all, though?'

Austin looked up at Ginny with vulnerable eyes, but then shrugged and looked away.

'Do you feel bad about it?' Ginny probed.

'Kinda.'

'He's not a very nice boy, is he? The boy you hurt.'

Austin shook his head.

'I get it. But do you think it's okay to stab someone with a pencil?'

'I don't know...Mom always says...' he trailed off.

'I know. Sting first.' Ginny sighed. She glanced at Austin and his glasses, and changed tack. 'Do you remember what Harry Potter's favourite spell is?'

'I don't think he has a favourite, they never talk about it if he does.'

'Okay, well, what spell does Harry use a lot whenever he fights the dark wizards?'

'Expelliarmus.'

'That's right. And Expelliarmus only disarms people, doesn't it?'

'Yeah.'

'And Harry uses that even when he fights Voldemort, right?'

'Yeah,' said Austin slowly, not sure what Ginny was implying.

Ginny leaned forward gently, meeting Austin's eyes with the kindest and least judging expression she could. She brushed his hair smooth with her hand.

'Do you think Harry would sting first?' she asked softly.

Austin looked at his shoes.

'No,' he choked out, and Ginny pulled him into her chest and hugged him tightly as he began to cry. 'Am I gonna go to Azkaban?'

'No, of course not,' Ginny soothed, rubbing his back. 'Everyone has bad days. It's like the Horcrux necklace in the last book, remember? You wear it and it makes y makes you say and do things that you wouldn't normally do.'

She pulled back and looked at Austin seriously.

'But I think we need to try and make sure that we can get through a bad day without hurting someone. And that's where therapy can help.'

Austin wiped his eyes and nodded. Ginny glanced at her phone, checking the time. She also checked her messages – still no response from her dad after she texted things going sideways.

'My friend's probably almost here. Will you go the therapy appointment?'

Austin nodded again.

'Okay, that's really good. Let's go wait outside, okay?'

She took Austin by the hand and, acting as naturally as possible, walked out into the hall and downstairs. Georgia – or Mary? That was something she hadn't had tim about yet – was in the kitchen tidying up. She seemed distracted, and kept taking long sips from a wine glass. A little early for that, Ginny thought. Georgia turned heard their footsteps.

'Where are you going?' she asked.

Ginny let her face fall back into anger; it was so easy when she wasn't really pretending.

'I'm taking Austin to the park. He needs cheering up,' Ginny lied, looking at her mother scathingly – it's your fault...Mary.

Georgia looked at Austin, his eyes red.

'Austin, baby, I'm sorry, I didn't mean to yell before.'

'You sent them away!' Austin yelled hotly, surprising both Ginny and Georgia, then he raced out the front door. Ginny followed, and she led him just out of sight of t where Georgia couldn't see so they could wait for Hunter.

He pulled up in his car a few minutes later, smiling at Ginny. Ginny tried to smile back as she jumped in, leaning back to check that Austin had put his seat-belt on.

'How you doing, buddy? I'm Hunter,' Hunter looked at Austin through the rear view mirror. Austin looked at him sulkily.

'It's been a hard day so far,' Ginny said apologetically. 'Austin, this is Hunter.'

Austin stared back.

'It's nice to meet you,' said Hunter, smiling encouragingly.

'Austin – isn't Hunter nice to pick us up? He's come completely out of his way to do this as a favour.'

'...thank you,' Austin said quietly.

86

Ginny and Hunter smirked at each other.

'Thank you,' Ginny said seriously. 'We wouldn't have been able to without you.'

'That's okay, I'm here for you.' He smiled fondly at her for a moment, then turned back to the road.

Ginny blinked. She'd just remembered. Max had told Hunter not to give up on Ginny yet. Ginny's insides squirmed with discomfort. Did he still like her? She risked him; he seemed up-beat, with a polite smile on his face. He didn't seem nervous. Surely he'd be kind of nervous, right? She dug her nails into her palms for the res trip.

She put her worries about Hunter out of her mind as they pulled up at the therapist office. She led Austin inside and directed him to sit in the warm waiting area, it friendly, unassuming yellow. Hunter politely sat near him, but not next to him. She approached the reception desk, where a kind-looking man was typing on a comp

'Um, hello,' Ginny said.

The man looked up and smiled at her.

'Hi, how can I help you?'

'Um, I'm bringing – um, my little brother has an appointment with Dr Darmody today. Should be under Austin Miller?'

'Austin...Miller...' said the receptionist, typing on his computer to access the file. 'Yes, I see, we have you at 2pm. Okay, first time here, yes?'

'Yes.'

The receptionist passed Ginny a clipboard and a pen.

'Fill these out with your brother, just standard patient information. I can see we already have your mother's permission form on file, so you guys are all set once th Ginny smiled politely, if not a little guiltily, and sat down between Austin and Hunter. She looked at the form and inhaled deeply. She was not stressed. She was not filled it in, pausing where it asked about a history of mental illness in the family. She checked 'Unknown'. She signed nervously under 'Guardian', and handed it bac with trembling fingers. Was she actually going to pull this off? She glanced at the entrance, half expecting Georgia to burst through and tackle her.

'Any minute now,' she said to Austin, sitting back with him.

'Can you come in with me?'

'Oh, um, I think you have to go in by yourself?'

Austin looked up at her in alarm.

'It's okay, it's okay. All you have to do is talk to them.'

'Austin Miller?' A kind voice called out.

Ginny looked up and saw a man in spectacles looking over the waiting room. She stood up and grabbed Austin's hand.

'Come on. It's okay.'

Austin trailed behind her shyly, hiding behind her legs. They walked up to Dr Darmody. Ginny smiled nervously.

'Hi, I'm Ginny. This is my brother Austin,' she gestured to the little head poking out by her side.

Dr Darmody gave a smile and crouched down to Austin's eye line.

'Hi Austin. I'm Dr Darmody.' He looked behind him down to his open office door and pointed. 'That's my office over there. Do you and your sister want to come in fo just hang out, get to know each other?'

Ginny squeezed Austin's hand encouragingly. He nodded. Dr Darmody smiled, standing back up to his full height, and led the way. Ginny glanced back at Hunter, w then followed Dr Darmody in. She was surprised to see his office was full of toys and life. The walls were adorned with finger painting artwork, there was what appe craft corner, and even musical instruments. She heard Austin let out a quiet 'whoa' from beside her. She sat Austin on a squashy couch and stood back awkwardly.

in a chair opposite and faced Austin.

'Ginny, you're welcome to sit too.'

She sat.

'So, Austin, it's really good to meet you. I can see you're a little nervous, so I think you're being very brave to come here.'

Austin smiled nervously.

'Do you know what therapy is?' Dr Darmody asked.

Austin nodded.

'Therapy is where you talk because you're worried.'

'Yeah, that's a pretty good way to explain it. What sort of things are you worried about, Austin?'

Austin looked up at Ginny.

'It's okay, you can tell him.'

'I did something bad.'

'Okay, do you want to tell me?'

'I hurt one of the kids in my class. With a pencil. I stabbed him in the hand because he was making fun of my mom and my family. And Mom says you should sting

'Okay. Is there anything else?' He looked kindly at Austin. Ginny was impressed – if he had been surprised by that information, it did not show at all.

'Mom sent away my secret cousin, too. And we just became blood brothers. And Mom and Ginny are always fighting.'

'Okay,' Dr Darmody said. He glanced over at Ginny, then back to Austin. 'Where is your mom today?'

'She's at home, she didn't want me to go to therapy because she's not worried. She says therapists are latte-drinking and tweed-wearing.'

Ginny swallowed and looked at the floor. Oh, no. She could feel Dr Darmody's eyes on her.

'Some of us definitely do drink lattes and wear tweed,' he said generously. He held his arms open and gestured to his clothes. 'Am I okay?'

Austin considered him, and his simple slacks and shirt.

'You're okay.'

Ginny couldn't help but smile as she watched Dr Darmody gently pry Austin out of his shell. He focused mostly on Austin, never once letting a single judgemental e his face. Occasionally he directed a question at Ginny, but he didn't ask about the consent form with Georgia's name on it.

After a while, Dr Darmody gave Austin an activity about anger to do. Anger is in all of us, he'd said, but it's not who we are and we can't let it control us. He armed array of pencils and crayons and asked him to draw anger as a person. Once Austin started, he stood up and looked at Ginny. Her stomach dropped. He gestured to of the room and she meekly walked over.

'Your mother doesn't know you're here,' he said in hushed tones.

It wasn't a question.

Ginny nodded, her chest tightening. Was he going to kick them out?

'What you've done is illegal. And I can't treat Austin. Under licencing laws, anyone under the age of twelve cannot consent to their own therapy and you have to be or a legal guardian to give that consent.'

Ginny looked up at him, and exhaled shakily. Was he going to call the police? Her nails found their way back into her palms. She was screwed. She'd been so stupid she was going to get caught.

'That being said, I believe Austin would benefit from therapy. Your mother definitely won't let him come?'

Ginny shook her head fervently, and to her embarrassment realised she was starting to tear up – from fear, from stress, the sheer volume of just everything that th overwhelm her at all times.

'Okay.' Dr Darmody glanced back over at Austin, who was using the colours red and black with abandon. 'What about yourself?'

'Me?' Ginny was surprised.

'Yes, I expect you would benefit from therapy as well. What you've done is very brave, and beyond your calling as an older sister – I think you also might need som Dr Darmody looked at her with compassion and understanding. Ginny shuddered and her tears fell. Dr Darmody wordlessly passed her a tissue from his desk and a smile before turning back to Austin to inspect his drawing of anger. Ginny stifled her affectionate chuckle – even from over in the corner, she could see it was going Dr Darmody told Austin to take his anger-wizard home and, if he ever felt the urge to sting first again, to tell the anger-wizard 'no'. He walked them out, dropping b receptionist to tell him there was no charge for their appointment and to mark it as a no-show. Ginny bit her lip; she'd stolen his time and made him complicit in a handed Ginny a business card.

'If you like, you can book an appointment with me yourself. If you don't have the support of your mother, we can discuss payment options.'

Ginny nodded and thanked him quietly.

Hunter took them home, parking a little way from the house again.

'Austin, you go on in,' Ginny said, handing him her keys.

She watched him safely walk around the corner and into their front yard before she turned to Hunter.

'I just wanted to say thank you...again.'

92

Hunter unbuckled his seat-belt and faced her. He smiled at her. And glanced at her lips.

Uh oh.

'It's really okay,' he said. 'Ginny, I wanted to tell you something...'

Ginny opened her mouth and started to shake her head.

'I know, I know' he said, before Ginny could get anything out. 'Don't be mad. Max told me, you're not ready. I just wanted to let you know that I'll be here when yo Ginny looked down. She had to be honest.

'Um, Hunter...'

Hunter reached out a hand and covered Ginny's.

'It's okay, you don't have to say anything now.' He rubbed her hand in what seemed like it was meant to be a comforting way.

Ginny felt a stab of annoyance – he hadn't really given her a chance to say anything. She extricated her hand.

'Thank you again – for the ride, and for sitting in the waiting room. I'm going to head in now.' She faked a smile at Hunter and left, waving as he drove away.

Ginny stared at her front door in trepidation. It felt strange and unusual. A third party observer – Dr Darmody – had confirmed that Ginny needed help. More than e acutely aware of her discomfort about her mother. Ginny resolutely walked forward, she could manage this – she'd done it so far. By the end of the day Austin was asked to stay with Ginny in her bed that night. He fell asleep as she finished off Alice in Wonderland for him.

All alone, Ginny had nothing to distract her from her musings on Georgia. Mary. Whoever she was.

8. Chapter 8

'Hey,' Marcus greeted Ginny at her locker. 'How did the rest of the weekend go?'

Ginny shut her locker and looked at him flatly.

'How do you think?' she sighed.

'Georgia still hasn't told you anything?'

'Nope. She's just running around pretending it's all normal. And she goes crazy if I try ask anything anymore.'

'Well, you got some stuff out of mystery aunt, right?'

'Some. Basically that Mom's right in keeping me from her parents. Which – fine, that may be true – it's the lying that I can't stand. I just want the truth. I don't thi unreasonable. I feel like I don't know who she is anymore.' She sighed and looked around at the school hall. 'I really don't feel like being here today.'

Marcus looked at her sympathetically and leaned against the row of lockers.

'Maybe you can do some digging.' He met her eyes conspiratorially. 'She'd be at work by now?'

Ginny smiled like she was caught with her hand in the cookie jar.

'I may have been thinking about ditching and going through her personal belongings.'

'Alright, let's go.'

'Really?'

'Yeah.'

And Marcus led the way out the door. Ginny rushed to catch up with him. She felt impatient, so they caught a ride-share home rather than walk. They stood united door for a moment; Ginny's home seemed surprisingly daunting when being entered with nefarious purposes.

'Wait in my room?' Ginny asked Marcus as they reached the upstairs landing. 'It's one thing for her daughter to violate her privacy, it's quite another for you.'

Marcus nodded and meandered over to Ginny's room, his hand brushing briefly on Ginny's waist as he left. Knowing he was there made Ginny feel oddly supported, continued into Georgia's room alone. She had a lump in her throat as she started peering into drawers. Bras, sex toys, ugh. Not quite what she was looking for.

Finally, hidden at the base of Georgia's closet, Ginny found a suspicious looking floorboard. Locating a nearby shoehorn, Ginny pried it upwards. Jackpot. Her heart pounding.

Photos from Georgia's childhood. Why does she keep it under here? A leather jacket. Odd. A gun.

A gun? Ginny's fingers trembled as she turned it over in shock. Was this real? It was heavy in her hands, and the cool metal unnerved her. Had her mother ever sho Ginny had never touched a gun before, and she wasn't sure she liked it.

Ginny heard the telltale click of a gun. Which was odd given that she'd never actually heard a gun in real life; regardless, she knew that noise as it appeared from b Someone was in the house, and in the room with her.

Lungs frozen, Ginny whirled around and brandished the gun she'd found, scrambling away from the assailant.

Mom?

'What the hell, Virginia?! What are you doing home?!' Georgia lowered the gun she had been pointing directly at Ginny.

Ginny hadn't heard that tone come from Georgia's mouth in so long; it was the voice she used when Ginny did something dangerous. The voice of fear. She sudden was reminded of when she was five and tried to pull a piece of toast out the toaster with a knife, and earlier when she was four and saw an interesting leaf on the r middle of traffic that she wanted to pick up and admire.

'I coulda killed you!' Georgia knelt down in front of Ginny, pulling the gun from her daughter's hand.

'I've never held a gun before.'

'What are you doing in here? Why you pawing through my closet?' Georgia began to hurriedly put away the hidden stash Ginny had uncovered.

'I want answers!' Ginny yelled, standing up. Indignation began to overtake the terror that had flooded her system.

'Answers to what?'

'All of it! Your past, everything! I'm sick of the lies.'

'I don't really care what you're sick of. You have no right to go through my stuff.'

'Don't talk to me about what is right. What is all this stuff? Why are there guns in the house? Why did you have to send Maddie away?'

'That's between me and Maddie,' Georgia sighed, getting up as she was done pushing all of her secret belongings back down into their hidden home.

'She's my aunt. Why couldn't I know that? They're my family.'

'They're not your family. I'm your family.'

'I just want you to be honest with me.'

'I have been honest!'

' Bullshit, Mary!'

In the time it took for Ginny to realise those words may have been a step too far for Georgia, it was too late.

Wham.

Georgia's hand had whipped out and smacked Ginny clean across the face with considerable force. It almost didn't hurt; Ginny's brain focused more on what seeme in information – her mother had just slapped her? That couldn't be right. Her mind went back over it, but no matter how it thought about it there was no other way had been hit. By her mother.

She placed a hand on her stinging skin and looked at Georgia in betrayal, confusion and hurt; she barely registered the expression of overwhelming surprise and re mother's typically composed face.

Ginny couldn't stop the tears that welled up and rushed out of the room, slamming the door behind her. She found Marcus standing awkwardly halfway across the h having come out to inspect the noise and hovering there, not wanting to intrude. His eyes locked in on Ginny's hand and the reddening skin beneath it. He frowned concern back at Georgia's closed door.

Ginny grabbed his hand and pulled him quickly back to her room, wrenching her door shut. She looked at her window, thinking of escape, and gasped as sobs sudd her body with a strength she didn't know they could. Marcus' arms were around her just as her legs gave-way beneath her, and they sank down to the floor.

Underneath Ginny's shock and numbness was a deep grief. Her relationship with Georgia would forever be split in two – the time before her mother hit her, and the Her lungs didn't seem to work, she breathed and gasped but the oxygen didn't seem to make it into her bloodstream. Gaping and choking, she gripped Marcus' arm desperately tried to inhale faster and faster. But her chest was frozen and her lungs continued to fail her. Oh god, she was going to die.

She needed her lighter.

'It's okay,' Marcus soothed, his voice sounding so very far away. 'Close your mouth, breathe in through your nose.'

She tried.

'Now hold it,' he whispered.

She tried, but her whimpers bled through her lips.

'It's okay, try again. Breathe in, and hold it for five seconds.' Marcus counted them for her. 'Now exhale.'

Ginny followed his instructions.

'Don't breathe in yet. Hold it... now breathe in.'

She latched onto his words, and found that air started returning to her. She shuddered a little, but she was breathing. Sometimes her ability to breathe would disap more, but Marcus gently calmed her.

After a few minutes, Ginny wiped her eyes.

'How'd you do that?'

'You had a panic attack. I've seen them before,' he shrugged.

Ginny took that in briefly.

'Can we go?'

'Yeah, I think we should.'

Ginny rose unsteadily and, without thinking, packed herself an overnight bag. She glanced at Marcus.

'Uh, can I stay at your place tonight?'

He nodded and turned to her window, opening it. He checked on Ginny quickly before he climbed out. Once he was gone, Ginny pocketed her lighter – just in case –

him out. On the top of the portico, she awkwardly pulled her window back down; it seemed prudent for some reason, like Georgia would be less likely to follow her perfectly capable of using the front door. With Marcus' help she got down to the ground and they dashed across to the Bakers' house.

'Marcus? What on earth are you doing home?' Ellen looked at the both of them in surprise. She had her bag and keys in hand and was midway through slipping on about to leave for work. She visibly took in Ginny's red eyes and the mark on her cheek.

She looked at Marcus, the blood draining from her face with an expression Ginny couldn't place.

'Did you hit her?' she choked out.

'No!' Marcus yelled, instantly infuriated.

Ginny shook her head.

'It was my mom.'

Ellen stared at Ginny.

'Come in, honey,' she finally said. She put her bag and keys down, and beckoned Ginny over to the table. Ginny sat weakly as Ellen fussed about her, inspecting he there's no cut or anything, so I don't think we need to disinfect. I'll get you an anti-inflammatory though.'

She paused by Marcus as she went to get the pill for Ginny. She placed a hand on his shoulder.

'I'm sorry, Marcus.' She gave him a quick hug. Marcus looked unamused over her shoulder.

'It's fine,' he muttered as she walked off.

Ellen came back with a pill and a glass of water. She sat in front of Ginny.

'I guess I did the right thing then, by not telling Georgia about you and Marcus?' She interlaced her hands on the table. 'I mulled over it for ages after that night yo But I thought maybe there was enough going on between you and your mom without adding Marcus to it, with what you told us.'

'Oh,' said Ginny. Truthfully, she'd kind of forgotten. 'Thank you.'

Ellen glanced at her watch, and sucked in air through her teeth. She looked anxiously at Ginny.

'Are you okay?'

'I'm okay...but can I stay here tonight? I don't think I can face my mom tonight...' Ginny nudged her overnight bag with her foot.

'Yes, but you're sleeping in Maxine's room.'

Ginny caught Marcus rolling his eyes in the background.

'How is that any better?' Marcus asked, seemingly to just be obstinate. 'Max like girls.'

'Well, Ginny doesn't,' Ellen retorted. She suddenly glanced doubtfully at Ginny. 'Right?'

'Yeah,' Ginny laughed.

Ginny's smile faded as she remembered Austin.

'Can Austin sleep here too?'

Ellen clicked her tongue.

'I guess he should. Do you think you're both in danger? Should we be calling the police?'

Ginny was taken aback, and then looked at her shoes.

'I – I don't think we're in danger. You should have seen her face after...she seemed more surprised than me.'

Ellen looked at Marcus.

'Did you see it?'

He shook his head. Ellen pursed her lips and looked back at Ginny.

'Are you sure?'

Ginny nodded.

'Okay...well, if you're okay, I'll go to work and we can sort it out when I get home. You can get set up in Maxine's room, maybe get some sleep. Marcus, you can go I'll drop you off.'

'What?' he protested. 'I'm not leaving her alone after that.'

But as much as he fought her, Ellen did not budge and she almost manhandled her reluctant son into her car, while he cast frustrated looks back at Ginny.

Left alone, Ginny sat on the floor by Max's bed and ignored the increasing number of incoming calls from Georgia, sending off a text to her dad instead.

G: Dad, it's getting really bad...

When he didn't respond shortly, she fished her lighter from her pocket and seared her thigh worse than ever before.

o

o - o

o - o - o

o - o

o

'Ginny!'

Max's loud voice woke Ginny partially up from her snooze on her belly, and then the full weight of Max unceremoniously landing on her back woke her up in full.

Max held onto Ginny's shoulders and placed her cheek against Ginny's.

'Are you okay? Marcus told me everything.'

'Yeah. Just sad,' Ginny said, her voice muffled a little by the pillow.

'Aw. I've been dying to come home since he told me, but if Mom made him leave, she definitely wasn't letting me go home early.'

'That's okay.'

Max shuffled down a little and rested her head on Ginny's back. Ginny could feel either tension or excitement in Max's body – she practically vibrated.

'Okay, so I know you're really sad right now and have every reason to be, but can I tell you something?'

'Sure.'

'I apologised to Sophie and we kissed and it was amazing!' she shrieked.

'That's awesome,' Ginny smiled. 'I'm glad.'

'You were so right about it, just be direct and truthful. It worked. So simple.'

'You know what they say...honesty is the best policy...'

Max made happy sounds.

'Hey...' said a quiet voice.

Ginny tried to glance up as Marcus' voice came from the door, but couldn't due to a Max-shaped log on her.

'Hey.' She lifted a clumsy arm and waved as best she could.

Marcus walked into her field of view and set next to her. He shot a disapproving look at Max, who half-heartedly smacked him away.

'Did you want to do anything?' he asked Ginny.

'Like what?'

'I dunno, eat? Watch a movie? Throw eggs at the neighbour house? Smoke?' He raised his eyebrows. 'All valid options.'

'Um...I'm tired...something low energy.'

'Movie?'

'Okay.'

'Loser, put on a movie for Ginny.'

'Fine, bossy.'

He gave Ginny a quiet smile, which she gave back, and then left. Max didn't move for a bit, still balancing on Ginny's back.

'He's nice to you,' she said solemnly.

Ginny nodded.

'You guys really are serious, aren't you?'

'I think so.'

Max sighed, and rolled off of Ginny. She pulled out her laptop and booted up something cheerful. Marcus came back a few minutes later with his own laptop and sa next to Ginny. It was a little squishy with the three of them.

'Marcus!' Max complained.

Marcus made a very rude gesture to Max that Ginny didn't need to know sign language to understand.

'Just because you two are going out, it doesn't mean you get to hang out with us all the time.'

'I know,' Marcus said simply, not looking up from his screen.

'Then why are you here?'

'Because Ginny wants me here.'

Max looked at Ginny, who nodded.

'Just today?' Ginny asked.

'In light of today's circumstances, yes.'

Marcus shot an annoyed look at Max after she'd turned away. He looked down at Ginny softly, who leaned over to rest against Marcus' legs.

Ginny tried to focus on the movie for a bit, but kept thinking of Austin. Austin who was so small and didn't understand what was happening. Austin who needed his Ginny abruptly sat up, surprising Marcus and Max. She pulled out her phone and called Georgia.

' Ginny, where are you? I want you to come home right now.'

'Mom, I was just calling to check in on Austin.'

' Austin is fine. Wondering where his sister is, but fine.'

'I want to come pick Austin up.'

' Look, I'm sorry I slapped you. Can you just come home so we can talk?'

'Can I pick him up?'

' No, he's here. With this mother. As he should be. As you should be.'

'So, no, then. That's what I'm hearing.'

' If you wanna see Austin, you'll need to come home.'

Ginny stared at her phone and hung up on Georgia. She inhaled deeply, closing her eyes. Marcus stood up and walked over.

'I'm going home,' she said to Marcus.

'Ginny, no,' Marcus said. 'After what she did? You should stay here.'

Ginny looked up at him, torn.

'I want to stay. But she won't let me pick up Austin, and I'm not leaving him alone with her.'

Max sat up on the bed and looked at Ginny sadly.

'Maybe we can break him out?' she asked.

'Look, she won't do it again. It's fine,' Ginny muttered, picking up her bag and pulling on her shoes.

She walked downstairs, Max and Marcus following her.

'How do you know?' Marcus asked.

Ginny shrugged.

'I just know. Besides, even if I thought she would, I'd still go back.'

'That's what concerns me,' said Marcus.

Ginny whirled on him.

'Would you leave Max?'

Max and Marcus involuntarily looked at each other, and pulled identical faces of resignation.

'Uh huh,' Ginny said knowingly.

Marcus sighed, and he took Ginny by her waist and pulled her in for a hug. Max groaned.

'Really, Max? Jeez,' Marcus said in disgust.

'Fine,' said Max. She waved her fingers dismissively.

Ginny pulled back and regretted looking into Marcus' eyes. He was reading her, scouring her for any flicker of doubt or insecurity. He'd never fixed her with a gaze s this one, and Ginny felt an appreciation for worried-Marcus.

Ginny brushed their concerns away and walked home.

Georgia at least looked sad and regretful as she apologised to Ginny. She gave her some lines about how if Ginny knew about Georgia's past...she'd never look at h and there wouldn't be any coming back from that. Ginny hid her anger, knowing that the mild swelling in her face marked the larger milestone that Ginny wouldn't from.

She hid Austin in her room with her, reading him a few chapters from a new book. She somewhat subconsciously placed Austin in bed furthest away from the door, between them if Georgia were to come in.

She kept her phone near her head and waited. He would call. It might take him a while, sometimes all day, but he would call. She could always depend on that.

More than ever, as the rocky ground of her relationship with Georgia crumbled, Ginny needed her dad.

Chapter 9

Ginny wiped the last stray remnant of birthday cake from her face and opened up the snapchat Hunter had just sent her.

Hunter's face filled her screen with his standard dog-filter.

' Happy birthday to you! Happy birthday to Ginnyyyyy!'

Ginny pursed her lips a little and put her phone back in her pocket before tugging at the parcel from her dad. She'd lugged the giant box from her dad upstairs and eyes of Georgia, and lifted it with difficulty onto her bed. As she pulled apart the cardboard of her birthday present, she was pleased to see a digital piano revealed a shiny red bow on the left-hand side.

'Wow,' she said, her hands brushing the surface of the keys.

'So what'd Zion get ya?' asked Georgia, who wandered up to Ginny's open door.

Ginny turned around, a little resentful, having intentionally secluded herself once Georgia passed the package over. She'd wanted this moment by herself – just her Ginny. Especially after Georgia had opened her card from her grandparents.

'A piano.' Her tone held a distinct note of pride.

Georgia walked in and appeared to inspect the gift with interest.

'You think this is good. Wait 'til you see what I got planned for tomorrow,' and she wiggled her eyebrows smugly at Ginny.

'Oh god. What does that mean?'

'It means tomorrow I planned a secret surprise,' Georgia smiled winningly.

'Oh goody, more secrets,' Ginny intoned sarcastically and glared at her mother, before clearing space on her desk and bodily lifting her piano over.

She plugged it in and sat down, experimentally playing out the sweet melody Zion had written just for her. She grinned at Georgia before she could help it.

'I still remember it.'

When Georgia gave her a smile back, Ginny's faded and she looked away again. She adjusted herself in her seat uncomfortably.

'Mom,' Ginny said, turning back to her piano and idly pressing some keys. 'Whatever you have planned...can we just not?'

'Why?'

Ginny's phone chimed, and she glanced at it, grinning as she read her text from Max announcing that Ellen and Clint would be away on the Saturday. She looked ba Georgia, her face growing unhappy.

'Because you didn't even ask me.'

'What? I can't give you surprises? Excuse me for caring!'

Ginny stood up, growing agitated.

'It's not like that. Did you think to ask me what I wanted? It's my birthday.'

'It won't be a surprise if I tell ya.'

'Don't you think I've had enough surprises recently?' Mary, she wanted to add, but didn't dare.

Georgia threw her hands up in frustration and stalked away. Ginny scoffed.

'Sure, just leave the conversation!'

Ginny watched her mother walk away, waiting for her to turn back around. But she didn't. Ginny rolled her eyes and finished getting ready for school, smoothing ou straight hair. There was a stab in her chest as she saw Dr Darmody's business card on her bedside table. Her gaze lingered on it, but she shook her head.

Ellen was kind enough to take Ginny in with Max and Marcus that day – who screamed excitedly and raised a confused eyebrow about Ginny's new hair respectively Georgia who stood at the front door. Ginny noticed how tight Ellen's smile was at Georgia and looked at her lap. Maybe she had been too rash in running to the Bak slapping incident.

Ginny, Max and Marcus walked together into school as Max begged Marcus to let her throw a party that Saturday for Ginny.

'Alright, I don't want the bro squad infiltrating our house, puking in our bathroom, killing my fish.'

'Okay, Brodie didn't kill your fish – he ate your fish,' Max pulled an expression like Marcus was stupid.

'You think it survived that trip, Max?'

'Come on! It's for Ginny, for her birthday. Just do it for Ginny.'

Ginny looked up at Marcus.

'I'm sorry about your fish,' she said.

'Yeah,' he said, looking like he'd rather not talk about it.

'Look, we don't have to...' Ginny murmured, her heart sinking.

'What? Yes, we do!' Max overrode Ginny. 'Come on, Marcus, you don't even have to be there.'

Marcus raised an eyebrow at Max, before his eyes landed squarely on Ginny.

'Oh, really?' He looked at her suspiciously, as they tested the new boundaries of their relationship.

Ginny bit her lip.

'You could come...?' she said hopefully, but was already reading the exasperated expression on Marcus' face and continued in defeat, '...and have a horrible time. I aren't really your thing.' She tucked some hair behind her ear.

'No, their parties aren't my thing.'

Ginny looked between Max and Marcus, both of whom she would like to see at her birthday celebration – her first birthday with friends. Real friends.

'Look, why don't we do something tonight instead?' Marcus asked.

Ginny nodded, trying to ignore an uncomfortable sensation in her belly, something bordering on nausea as her love for Max and her love for Marcus mixed like oil a

'And then you can bring over the worst people in the world,' Marcus said to Max, who jumped up and down excitedly. Marcus then left the two of them, but not befo leaning over to give Ginny a kiss on the cheek – who grinned in response.

'Wow, lame kiss,' scoffed Max. 'Prudes.'

'Quiet, you.' Ginny put a disapproving hand over Max's mouth and pushed her away playfully. 'We're taking it slow now; this is big for both of us.'

'I know, but my god, you're glacial. You're humans, not continents. You can move more than like an inch every century. I dunno how fast continents move. But fast guys. I think that's the first time I've seen you do anything but look at each with goo-goo eyes at school.'

'We're thinking of your eyes,' Ginny said with mock generosity.

'Oh, so kind. I will erect a statue in both your honors.'

'Don't say erect when talking about your brother.'

'EW, GINNY!'

After a brief visit from Sophie, Ginny was delighted to find that the rest of MANG had decorated berry tree for her birthday.

'I'm just so happy that you moved here, you know,' said Max, placing a plastic tiara on Ginny's head. 'I don't know what I would have done without you. It would h Drake and Josh, but no Josh. You know, like just Drake. But not Drake Drake. Drake! We should all go to a concert together,' Max said gleefully.

'Ha ha ha ha, okay, yeah we get it, Max.' Abby started, sounding and looking exhausted. 'You know, Ginny's the best. You're amazing, you're the best. And I'm just over it. And I,' she inhaled sharply, 'I have to go to class.'

And she strode away. Ginny blinked after her.

'That was hateful,' said Norah, completely non-plussed.

'Pretty bitchy,' agreed Max.

'Maybe she just has something going on – like at home or something?' Ginny suggested subtly.

'Or she's just insanely jealous. She's become The Grinch Who Stole Sophomore Year. I can't,' Max flopped down on the berry tree chair. Ginny hoped her face didn't knew about Abby's home struggles.

Jordan appeared at Norah's side.

'Hey, guys. I'm supposed to tell you all to look in that general direction.'

And they did, Ginny smiling at Marcus who was seated in the red section nearby, her belly clenching as he smirked back. Ginny shared a glance with Max as music over the loud speakers in the hall. Hunter soon stepped out from one of the other corridors and began to tap dance in time to the music, which slowly revealed itse adaptation of Happy Birthday.

Her friends whooped around her. Ginny's mouth fell open and she tried to process what was happening, Abby's outburst flying out of her mind. Hunter smiled at he with himself. Ginny laughed joyfully as Hunter slowly got closer, with a few more students joining in as he progressed, and felt a peculiar note of pride and validatio Ginny noticed Marcus looking at Hunter with disgust.

114

Hunter was getting closer and as the song flourished to a finish, he extended a hand out to Ginny. She caught Marcus' eyes, who looked back at her dubiously, but Hunter anyway who twirled her towards him and tipped her ceremoniously. Ginny laughed and Hunter pulled her back up-right. That was nice.

'Happy birthday, Ginny!' Hunter yelled

Ginny smiled, but looked immediately over to Marcus, whose expression had grown dark. She stepped back from Hunter uncomfortably for Marcus' sake.

'That was very nice, thank you.'

Hunter pulled her into a hug.

'Anything for the birthday girl!'

Ginny pulled back as politely as she could, looking again over to Marcus, who was starting to stand up.

'Hunter, that was so sweet of you, but I have to go.' She turned, briefly saying 'Love you, mean it!' to Max and Norah before catching up with Marcus.

She ignored hearing Hunter audibly say 'What?' behind her.

'Uh, hey,' she said, falling into step alongside Marcus.

'Hi.'

Ginny took in his stony voice.

'Um, what's wrong?'

'You haven't told Hunter yet.'

Ginny pouted.

'I'm going to. I promise.'

'It's just – I already have to have him in my house on Saturday. I'm not going to also watch him flirt with my – my, uh. You. With you.' He blinked a few times, clea before pasting an unassuming expression on his face.

Ginny bit back a smile.

'I promise, I wasn't flirting back. I just haven't found a good time to tell him.' Ginny continued to let Marcus lead her further from her next class. 'And I'll tell him th my boyfriend...? But you are...something.'

Marcus shrugged noncomittally. Ginny sighed.

'Okay, I think we're going to have to define things at some point.'

'Why? Labels are stupid.'

'Orrrr they're very helpful when explaining your relationship to someone.'

Ginny stepped in front of Marcus, causing him to stop walking.

'Are you my boyfriend?' she asked directly.

Marcus stared at her.

'I'm not your boyfriend,' he said firmly. 'But I'm not...unlike a boyfriend.' He seemed to be choosing his words carefully.

'What do you think being a boyfriend is?' Ginny asked. 'What's the actual issue here?' Anxiety started to gnaw in Ginny's stomach.

'It's just...it's so fake. Boyfriends and girlfriends, and Facebook official,' he said, his eyes rolling so far back in his head Ginny was concerned she might never see th then it only lasts two weeks, and suddenly there's a new official boyfriend. Useless labels for shit that doesn't even matter.' He gestured behind him. 'And I'm never anything like that.'

'Oh,' Ginny said, glancing down at her hands. 'But you haven't changed your mind about me?' She looked back up, trying to keep her face steady.

Marcus looked at her with a kind of haughty amusement, and firmly kissed her on the lips. Ginny's heart raced, and she glanced around all flustered at the people w There was at least one passerby whose eyes had widened in surprise. Ginny smiled at her shoes, pleased.

'I don't want you to think that I'm not serious about you though,' Marcus said.

'Me too,' said Ginny. 'About you,' she added, grinning. He grinned back and Ginny's heart soared. 'But, duly noted. No tap number from Marcus.'

Marcus glanced over his shoulder at the halls that were starting to clear. He looked back at Ginny.

'Wanna cut?' He jerked his head at the nearest exit.

Ginny took his hand and escaped from it all, for just a little.

o

o - o

o - o - o

o - o

o

Ginny ignored her latest text from Hunter, not even opening it to read the full message. The preview of it seemed to be talking about tomorrow's party. She put her and turned her attention back to her shiny new piano.

She sang out her father's words.

' And I can see my face...' '

Her phone chimed again.

M: Hey, can I come over now? [Window emoji]

G: Sure. I'm in my room

No sooner had Ginny put her phone back down and pressed a piano key than Marcus was sliding her window up and crawling through.

'Oh, hello. Forgot that you were asking permission until just before coming in, did you?' Ginny smirked.

He smiled charmingly at her.

'Howdy, neighbor.'

'Nice dodge. It's okay, I did the same.'

'You got a piano?'

Marcus leaned over her and began playing a one-handed jazz riff. Ginny stifled her impressed face and the now-familiar swoop in her belly from being in close-quar Marcus.

'I didn't know you played piano.'

'Just a little.'

'Hmm.'

'Uhh...' Marcus' charming facade suddenly faded as he pulled something from his back pocket. 'Happy birthday.'

He went to hand Ginny a rolled up sheet of paper. Ginny was pleasantly surprised.

'You didn't have to get me any-'

He jerked it away from her reach, smiling like a brat.

'-thing.'

He proceeded to offer and rescind the scroll a number of times, while Ginny tried to accept it.

'Okay. Yeah. No?' Ginny giggled as he toyed with her, before finally relinquishing it. She laughed and rolled off the rubber band and unfurled the paper.

She was shocked and touched to find a gorgeous water-colour portrait of herself. She suddenly realised that Marcus must have painted the eye on his bedroom wal some reason she'd assumed his well-off parents had hired someone to do it. She took in how beautiful yet solemnly he had captured her, somehow displaying fragil simultaneously. It was so special.

'I painted it,' Marcus added somewhat unnecessarily.

Ginny nodded.

'Marcus, thank you. I love it.'

The words didn't come close to how much she appreciated the piece of art. She stood up and hugged him, pulling him tightly to her, hoping the way she squeezed h portray the deep gratitude she felt – for him, his art, for this intimate moment they shared, for Marcus putting brush to paper and proving that he saw her – saw he arms held her tightly back. They both began to breathe a little deeper from the prolonged contact and Ginny pulled her head back to kiss him, her mind blurred. Sh badly – the very particular sensation that Marcus gave her. It was excitement and contentment all at once, a calm sense of stillness at her core, a deep knowledge accepted and seen. Appreciated. Loved. No agenda. Exactly as she was. She suddenly wished her hair wasn't straight at the moment.

Ginny longed for Marcus, a deep yearning low in her body. She placed her hands on the back of his head as their kiss deepened naturally, and all things Marcus inva

– his lips, his tongue, the hands that pulled at her shirt, and the length of his body pressed into hers. Her shirt was lifted over her head, and then Marcus' jacket an gone too. She pulled him down to her bed. It took all her strength not to rip off her pants.

Slower this time, she reprimanded internally, even as her body and mind screamed at her that this was the incorrect lesson to have learned.

Marcus situated himself between her legs, also not making any attempts on his own pants. Ginny smiled into their kisses, as her legs hooked around his hips. She g Marcus pressed himself against her through his clothes, and she became very aware of Marcus' keen interest in the situation. Oh god, how she liked to feel wanted He pulled gently away from their kiss, their lips barely brushing as he gazed directly into her eyes instead. He did it again and Ginny's breath hitched, in a very goo hand found Ginny's and he intertwined their fingers, pushing their hands firmly into her bed. Marcus began to find a rhythm, never taking his eyes from Ginny, exce her mouth and gauge her reactions. Ginny's blood thundered in her head as they breathed each other in, and she wanted so badly to remove their remaining clothe would mean stopping. And she wanted even more to not stop.

When Ginny accidentally let out a quiet moan, she brought her free hand to her mouth, glancing with fearful eyes at her closed door, and Marcus abruptly stopped, his own shoulder. When no one came bursting through, she looked back at Marcus, who seemed to be taking great pains not to look too pleased with himself. Ginny eyes at him playfully.

'Maybe we should wait...' Ginny said, sighing. 'Your parents won't be at your house tomorrow...?'

'Uh huh,' Marcus said, but he leaned down and kissed her again, his body resuming its pattern.

Ginny pulled Marcus in tightly with her legs. All she could hear was their breath, and the blood that pumped ferociously in her mind. Marcus, it seemed to chant as Marcus. How loved she felt, how wanted. His skin burned hers, and Ginny could only want more as suddenly he was reaching around her back to unhook her bra.

121

Marcus. Marcus. Marcus.

They both paused to hurriedly undo their pants, some silent communication passing between them that there would be no stopping that night, and scooted under h quietly and quickly.

Marcus. Marcus. Marcus.

Their lips rejoined as if apart for an eternity, and Marcus' hand was between her legs. He seemed pleased at what he found, as he grinned against her lips before ki eagerly, his excited breath loud in her ear.

Ginny also reached down to touch Marcus, not really sure what to do – suddenly realising through her hazy mind that she'd only touched him once – very briefly –

first unplanned rendezvous. Marcus dropped his forehead against her shoulder in response, his breath growing deeper. She listened for clues, and as she remember time Marcus did this for her, she was inspired to wet her hand, pushing aside Marcus' hand on her momentarily to do so. The sudden gasp Marcus gave when she re it was a good decision.

But none of this was enough. She wanted more of that feeling. In her body, yes, but her mind – her mind was on fire and she wanted this high to last as long as it They breathed each other in as if they themselves were oxygen, and their kisses became rough and hard. At some point, a switch flicked inside both of them, and t joyfully, painstakingly gave themselves to one another.

Ginny felt as if she soared. His touch gave her flight; she was amongst the clouds as every flex of his body and every second of the almost mind-numbing delight o connected to someone took her further and further away. She wasn't in her bedroom, there was no unwanted Mayor in her kitchen with her secret-identity mother.

far away from the rest of the world and the troubles that plagued her, to where she existed as light and wind, skipping freely from moment to moment. She was the sunset on water, she was dandelion puffs on an inexorable whirlwind.

She was Ginny. Just Ginny. And she was happy.

Chapter 10

The first thing Ginny had done when she woke up was smile.

She'd pulled her covers over her head and privately grinned, feeling small quivers all over her body as if her muscles couldn't take feeling so happy. She'd recounte in her mind, savouring her memories. She and Marcus might have royally screwed up their first sexual encounter, but had completely made up for it that time.

Her lips were sensitive, and she'd lightly brushed her tongue over them, still dainty from firm kissing. There had been a tenderness on her neck from Marcus' mout ached almost luxuriously. All of them Marcus. Little traces of Marcus. Lingering moments of leftover sunshine.

She'd rolled over to her phone, wanting to send a good morning text to him.

Oh.

She'd forgotten.

Yesterday

H: I hope you're keen for your party

tomorrow.

I've got a special surprise for the best

birthday girl!

Ginny had frowned. She needed to tell Hunter, and soon, about the incorrect information Max had so innocently passed on to him. But not over text.

Today

G: Awesome, can't wait

She'd pursed her lips uncomfortably. Was she lying or not? On the one hand, she had enjoyed his dance. It was fun. It was also brief; the kind of surprise where if least it's over quickly. But it felt nice, that Hunter organised something like that for her. Although it was public. Very public. An unbidden smile forced its way throug many people could say someone had done a tap dance in public for them?

She'd opened up her text thread with Marcus and was pleasantly surprised to see three dots, showing that Marcus was currently typing to her. She'd smiled and wa M: Is it dumb if I miss you already?

G: Yeah, you dummy

and no. I miss you too

M: Cool, both dumdums

G: Who you calling a dumdum,

dumdum?

He'd sent a snoozy selfie, his hair and eyes clearly showing he'd just woken up, with sloppily handwritten font saying 'u r a dum'. Ginny had laughed and sent a self

'no u'.

It had been such a lovely morning. If only she hadn't needed to pee.

'You excited for your big sweet sixteen surprise today?' Georgia asked as Ginny sat down at the table for breakfast.

'Gosh, Mom, I don't know,' Ginny deadpanned. 'I had such a fun first surprise already when the mayor was naked in my bathroom.'

Ginny's frustration and anger with her mother seemed to know no bounds. Georgia had been seeing Paul for, what – two weeks? And he was already sleeping over.

just stabbed a kid in the hand and her mother was already acting like it hadn't happened. Mary had slapped and pointed a gun at Ginny only a few days ago. How c act like everything was okay?

What would Dr Darmody say...?

Hiding a mischievous grin, Ginny began to callously list some of the many names making up Georgia's ex-boyfriend roster under the guise of casual conversation, g on it. Paul, a gentleman – outwardly at least, changed the subject.

'So, I hear your mom has quite the big day planned. Are you excited?'

'Not really,' she said, smiling at him sweetly, satisfied at the sour expression on Georgia's face.

The doorbell rang.

'I got it,' Georgia said mysteriously, rising from her chair and practically gliding over to the front door. Ginny waited like one condemned for her birthday surprise to When Max, Norah and Abby walked in and yelled 'surprise', Ginny's expression fell even further and her teeth clenched. She burned with anger. In her own house?

really going to pull this in front of Ginny's friends.

Ginny stared at the bright, congenial faces of her friends who were so pleased to have kept this little secret from her. Ginny's worlds were mixing.

But it had been such a nice morning.

o

o - o

o - o - o

o - o

o

After a quasi-enjoyable day with her friends and a visit from the incomparable Avril Vagine, Ginny shushed her friends as they began to sneak out the window. Onc crouched on the portico roof, Ginny instructed Max and Norah, the tallest, to go first.

'Great,' Ginny said, as they landed on the ground gracefully. 'Now you have to help me and Abby get down.'

Max and Norah stifled their laughter as Ginny lowered herself down as much as she could, her legs wiggling helplessly in the air in front of them.

'Ginny, Ginny,' Max said breathlessly, as she grabbed Ginny around the waist. 'Smile.'

Ginny looked down in time to see Max take a horrifically-angled selfie of the two of them. Max put her phone away and helped Ginny down.

'You delete that right now.'

'No, this will be a beautiful memory,' Max simpered.

After Norah helped Abby down, they ran as silently as four excited teenage girls could across the road. Safely ensconced inside the Bakers' home, Max began to set and texted all the other invitees that the party was a go. Ginny excused herself to go visit Marcus, tugging at her white top.

She found him on his bed, sketching on an art pad. He glanced up when she walked in, his eyes severely bloodshot and unfocused. He glanced at her clothes, or he wasn't sure, but she allowed that sense of stasis to envelop her. Warm. Calm. Marcus.

'Save some for me?' she asked, hopping next to him on the bed. She leaned over and kissed him.

He didn't answer, but turned over to his ashtray, re-lit his joint and inhaled hard. He then pulled Ginny in for a kiss and breathed the smoke into her lungs. Ginny p surprise, coughing it all out. He grinned at her.

'Sorry, I see that was new for you,' he laughed. He handed her the joint itself so she could freely partake. 'So how long until I have to batten down the hatches?'

'Fifteen or twenty minutes,' she said, taking a hit.

'Hmm.'

He put his art pad aside and pulled Ginny in for a more serious kiss. Ginny tingled with another amazing feeling, her chest tight and excited like it contained a blow She may have held a literal drug in her hand, but Marcus was the one she chased. Her hand hovered awkwardly in the air, hesitant to move the smoking joint anyw Marcus' bedspread or his body. He pushed her downwards, mouthing on her neck, and down to her exposed belly.

Ginny gasped and gently pushed him away.

'Your door is wide open.'

'Ah.' He stood up and closed it, leaning against the door to do so, with an almost predatory look on his face as he gazed at Ginny. She swallowed in response.

'The rest of MANG are right downstairs,' she said, as Marcus came back and kissed her exposed belly again and began to undo her pants. He looked back up at her.

'We can stop if you want?' he asked.

Ginny looked away with a small smile on her face.

'Don't get bashful on me now,' he laughed.

' Wanting to stop isn't necessarily the right word. Shush,' she added as Marcus adopted a very smug expression, and leaned over to Ginny's hand to inhale from the between her fingers. Ginny took another hit herself afterwards, but nodded encouragingly, unable to resist chasing the happiness. 'We'd have to be quiet.'

'Well, that's up to you,' he shrugged, undoing her fly casually.

'And quick.'

Marcus pulled her pants and underwear off.

'Well, I dunno, this is my first time trying this, so I dunno how I'll good I'll be.' He pulled Ginny towards the edge of the bed so that her legs hung off, and knelt dow her.

First time? Ginny looked at him confused – and then suddenly was not confused at all as Marcus kissed her again – between her thighs.

Ginny was not prepared. Her eyebrows knit together; conflicted, she knew she should feel good, but a remarkably peculiar sensation blasted Ginny – she was in he her body. She was cold, and her body alien. These were not her limbs. This was not her body.

For some reason, her mind flashed with the face of Kenny, her late step father.

How did she normally move? With a conscious effort, she surreptitiously trailed a hand down – somehow it was her hand – and rested the palm on the flesh of the thigh, hiding the raised skin of burn marks. Perhaps Marcus had not noticed before, but he had a very different view now. Ginny tried to concentrate, or relax, she w lungs froze in the chest that Ginny objectively knew was hers. She forced it to breathe. What if he saw? What if he saw?

129

Marcus stopped and looked up at Ginny.

'What's wrong? Do you want me to stop?'

From her remote room in the depths of her mind, she found she could still speak.

'Um,' she managed. She could see Marcus fighting through the marijuana-fuelled haze, his concern growing greater. Ginny tried to pull the legs together; they were almost non-responsive, but she managed to bring knees to rest against one another. Marcus awkwardly backed away from her.

He handed Ginny her underwear and pants, which she took absently, and clumsily put them on.

'Um, I'm sorry.' He pushed his hair back in confusion and looked at her at length. He raised a hesitant finger and pointed it in the vague direction of her house. 'We sex last night, right? I'm not just super high?'

Something about that question snapped Ginny back into control of her body. Ginny took in his face for a moment, scrutinising. He looked back at her, the very esse confusion. Not passive aggressive, she determined.

'Marcus, you smoke too much if you honestly have to ask that.' She re-arranged her clothes, pulling down where her shirt had lifted.

She put Ginny away for a moment; the thing that looks like Ginny coming out in her stead.

Masked. Protected.

'That's probably true. But what's wrong?'

'Nothing.' She helped him up off the floor and pecked him on the cheek. 'I better get back downstairs and finish setting up.' She turned about and made to leave.

'Ginny?'

His voice, quiet and worried, ran through her like a blade, stopping her in her tracks towards the door.

The mask was not designed to keep out Marcus Baker.

'You didn't do anything wrong,' she said calmly as she turned back. Very polite. Non-confrontational. She wished he didn't look at her so earnestly, as she carefully features into an expression of standoffishness.

'But something's wrong.'

Ginny said nothing. Marcus put his fingers over his eyes and then stretched the skin out, groaning a little.

'Ugh, I'm too high for this. Are – are you okay?' He gestured at her; this seemed to focus him a little.

She smiled in a way she knew that came across kindly, and walked back over to give him a gentle hug.

'What are you doing?' he asked, pulling back and placing his hands squarely on her arms.

'What do you mean?' she blinked. Innocence.

He waved a hand in the general area of her face.

131

'That's my face,' she deadpanned, and anxiety ruffled just below the veneer of her composure.

Marcus looked at her sourly.

'That's not your face.'

Ginny blinked, and Marcus sighed.

'You don't have to tell me anything. But don't lie to me.' He sat down on his bed and pulled his sketch back over, quietly adding some more lines to the page. She w Ginny stood awkwardly, hoping Marcus' frown would ease and he'd look back up, perhaps resigned but no longer frustrated with her. He continued to draw, and Gin sank; it landed somewhere around her knees. Her chest tightened in a bad way, like it closed in on itself. Shrunken and small without the active glow of Marcus' go There arose great raucous greetings from downstairs.

'Bro squad's all here,' Marcus intoned. 'You go enjoy your party.'

'Marcus...'

'Ginny, not right now.'

Suddenly furious, Ginny whipped around and stomped out, pulling the door shut behind her. Damn Marcus. Ginny was not going back in there. She made her way d joined the party.

'Birthday girl!' Hunter cried out, enveloping her in a hug.

Taken by surprise, Ginny smiled for real. She hugged him back. Warm. Not Marcus-warm. But still – warm.

'It's not even her birthday anymore,' said Press, who was at the table pouring himself a drink.

'Thanks,' said Ginny pointedly, giving Press a little side-eye.

'Ah, but she's still the party honoree.' Hunter pulled back and grinned widely at her. It didn't fill her like Marcus' smile did. But she liked that he was smiling at her.

'Hey Ginny, happy birthday!' called Sophie from over where Max had hugged/assaulted her in the doorway.

'Beirut!' Brodie yelled, where he had just finished setting up a bunch of plastic cups.

Ginny and Abby teamed up against Hunter and Press, wishing to lose because it gave Ginny the excuse to drink up, each time she tipped her head back draining a confusing anger at Marcus away and trading it with the fuzziness of being tipsy. This was her party, and she would have a good time. Marcus or no Marcus.

However Ginny and Abby made quite a team and proceeded to wipe the floor with Press and Hunter, but there was enough of an alcoholic glow about her to assuag frustration. Abby lifted and spun Ginny in celebration.

'Ginny!' Brodie almost roared at her. 'Birthday girl looking fire with that new hair!'

'Mm, thank you!' Ginny said playfully, swishing her straightened locks.

'I like it way better this way.'

Oh, no.

'If only you had an ass, you'd be perfect,' Brodie continued, completely oblivious. 'It's weird that you don't, but...' He tipped his head to the side casually, as if it wa disconcerting to him that Ginny's butt was the disappointingly small size it was.

Ginny narrowed her eyes at him.

'Excuse me?'

She wasn't sure if it was the alcohol, or her halfhearted argument with Marcus, but Ginny was suddenly very ready to fly off the handle. She stared Brodie down, w backtrack or double down, tense like a loaded catapult.

Hunter appeared beside her.

'Dude, just... - christ, man,' Hunter said, shaking his head, as if he couldn't believe what had just come out of Brodie's mouth.

Ginny couldn't tell if Hunter's assistance bothered her further.

'What?' Brodie asked, as Ginny walked away.

She just wanted to enjoy her birthday party. Her first real birthday party!

Her firm footsteps grew louder as she walked away from the music. She realised her feet were leading her upstairs to Marcus' room. She paused on the upstairs lan his closed door. She doubted that he wanted to see her.

'Hey,' said Hunter, who had followed her upstairs. 'You okay?'

Ginny turned to face him.

134

'He's a jerk.'

'Yeah, he was.'

Ginny strode forward, bypassing Marcus' bedroom and towards the guest bedroom. She sat heavily on the nicely made-up bed, and flopped backwards. She remem needed to tell Hunter about Marcus and sat up. For some reason it seemed too provocative to be lying down. Hunter sat on the bed with her, and they crossed their one another.

'I'm so sorry about Brodie. I know he's my friend and all, but...honestly, I don't even think he knows I'm Taiwanese. Like I'm just all of Asia to that guy. I'm Thailan They kept it light, chuckling a little, keeping the rumbling disturbance beneath the surface.

'Yeah. No, I'm white, I'm black. It depends on who you ask and what song is playing.'

'Yeah. No, I'm not Taiwanese to Asian folks. No. Then I'm white.'

'I love it when they piece it all together and get really gross and excited like, " What are you?" ' '

' " What are you?" ' Hunter said back, eyes wide.

'I have no frickin' clue,' said Ginny, and she played with the bedspread.

'I know what you are,' said Hunter.

'Hmm?'

'You're beautiful.'

135

Ginny couldn't help it, she laughed. So cheesy. She cleared her throat.

'Sorry, that was sweet.'

Admittedly, it pleased her to hear Hunter say that. But she thought of Marcus, which panged her heart. She knew she should feel bad because Hunter liked her, and really like him back, but it was just so nice to be liked. And Hunter was easier, in a way. It was light and breezy. It didn't have the undercurrent of a storm like Marc no risk.

She really needed to tell Hunter about Marcus. The heavy weight of reluctance cemented her mouth.

'Do you want your special surprise now?' Hunter asked. 'I was going to give it to you in front of everyone, but now I think...maybe just the two of us?'

'Oh,' said Ginny. 'I forgot. Sure.'

Hunter stood up quickly.

'I'll go get it.'

'Wait,' Ginny said. She couldn't let Hunter give her a present and then sort-of-not-really break up with him right afterwards.

'What?' he asked, halfway out the door.

Ginny looked at him, heart beating rapidly. She thought of Marcus' stony face, the cool way he had ended their conversation, and the sudden risk of loss that Marcu Hunter smiled politely while he waited, unassuming.

'...Could you get me a drink while you're down?'

136

'Sure,' he grinned, and raced downstairs.

Left alone with herself, Ginny tried to ignore the thoughts knocking on her mind. She stared at the plain bed covers.

Don't use Hunter.

He likes it, he wants it like this.

Hunter deserves better.

She kind of liked Hunter.

Don't lie.

Marcus probably doesn't love her anymore.

Don't be stupid, he said he loved her just last night.

That was before.

That was before.

That was before.

It started to grow all too loud. Ginny's mind was a cyclone, thoughts chasing one another like snapping dogs.

She wanted Marcus.

But she wouldn't go to him. She wanted her lighter. Ginny's nails dug into her palms; she distantly realised it had been a little while since she'd done that.

Ginny stood up, intending to run to the bathroom, but Hunter was back at the door.

'Sit down,' he grinned, handing Ginny a drink.

She fixed a smile to her face and sat back down. She sipped her drink. It wasn't very strong, that was no good.

Hunter pulled his guitar from behind back. Ginny raised an eyebrow. Hunter sat down on the bed next to her, spent a moment arranging his phone on the bedside t a pick from his pocket. He cleared his throat.

'I'm not really a singer,' he prefaced, looking Ginny mock-seriously in the face. Ginny nodded in return faux-seriousness.

'Are you going to sing Happy Birthday now? What medium will you do next? A Happy Birthday dramatic reading?'

Hunter laughed.

'No, not Happy Birthday. I, uh, actually wrote this a little while ago.'

'Oh, an original.'

Hunter smiled and looked away as he strummed the first chord.

' I can barely breathe when you are near.

And I'm really, really, really scared you're gonna disappear.'

Ginny's smile faded as she listened.

' I can't breathe when you are near.'

Hunter looked back up at her, and for the first time ever, Ginny thought she saw just a hint of vulnerability on his typically confident face.

' I don't know how to tell you.

There's a million things I want to say.

From the moment I met you my heart grew.

And I think of you every day.

I can barely breathe when you are.

My life was in the darkness and you suddenly appeared.

You say words that I wanna hear.

I can barely breathe when you are near.

You're everything and more to me.

It's all I wanted you to know.

And if I hold you tightly, I'll never let you go.

I can't breathe when you are near.

And I really, really wanna drown your worries and your fears.

With you, I cry no tears.

And I can barely breathe when you are near.'

As his last strum faded away, Ginny swallowed. That was nice.

'Was...was that about me?' Ginny needed confirmation.

Hunter nodded.

'I think you're amazing. I really like you.' He looked over at the direction of the door, as if he needed a brief moment. 'Look, I know you need time.'

Ginny bit the inside of her lip a little.

'But I want to be your boyfriend.'

God, it was just so easy with Hunter. Everything on the table. "I want to be your boyfriend", boom. And in that moment, Ginny wanted to want Hunter. She wanted guy that was so easily and so openly wanting to be with her, one of her friends, a natural extension of the group she'd found herself in. The guy that would be at he party. Not the guy hidden in his bedroom.

Hunter glanced at her lips.

Yes.

No.

Just once.

But Marcus.

As Hunter began to lean in, Ginny was disconcerted. It was wrong. It wasn't Marcus. Hunter's kind eyes approached, a gentle smile on his lips. She wished the eyes intense, wished his lips were serious with his need for her, longed for stray locks of hair falling across a forehead, and for hands that gripped her.

He wasn't Marcus.

But he wanted her.

Ginny stood on a precipice. Heart pounding, she knew she had only a moment to make a choice. Hunter inched closer. It would be so easy – just stand up, or put a shoulder and hold him back. Say 'I'm sorry, Hunter, but I'm not really into you and I'm really into Marcus'.

But the split second ticked away, and Hunter's lips pressed softly on Ginny's. She closed her eyes in a pale imitation of enjoyment. There was no swoop in her belly a deep satisfaction in feeling wanted. Hunter placed a hand on the back of her neck, and Ginny allowed him to pull her a little closer. He placed a hand on her waist Ginny's mind was thoroughly occupied with idle thoughts, like how odd kissing could feel, or how Hunter's fingers were a little calloused on her skin. It was all empt muscular. Completely without passion. But she allowed her lips to lie.

Her mouth tasted of Hunter and gratification, slaking a thirst for validation intrinsically built inside her that Ginny was terrified to realise existed.

When Hunter pulled back and smiled happily at her, it all disappeared, and Ginny felt slapped with the contrast.

She was Ginny again.

Empty.

And a fucking disgrace.

Chapter 11

Ginny was having trouble processing the happiness on Hunter's face with the avalanche of guilt that had collapsed on her. The cocktail of alcohol and marijuana in her system revolted against her, and her stomach lurched uncomfortably.

What had she done.

In one fell swoop of misplaced lips she'd betrayed Marcus, and used and led on Hunter.

Hunter turned over to his phone on the bedside table and fiddled with it while Ginny fought the urge to cry or vomit. Or both.

The tinny audio of a phone speaker rang out in the bedroom. Ginny's head snapped up, and saw Hunter had captured his serenade on camera. Hunter brought it ov

'Look, how good is this?' He grinned as 2-minutes-ago Hunter sang out his kindly thought out lyrics.

Time slowed down for Ginny as she saw Hunter pop-up a menu on his phone to share the video to social media.

'No!' she yelled, panicked.

Hunter glanced at her in confusion.

'What?'

'Please don't upload that,' she begged, her eyes wide as Hunter's thumb hovered dangerously close to selecting the YouTube app.

'What? Why?' His thumb didn't move away.

'Because! This was...private,' Ginny improvised.

'Don't you want people to see? I worked really hard on that song.'

'Well, I'm in the video too. And I'm uncomfortable about it.'

'Oh.' Hunter frowned, and clicked out of the 'share' menu on his phone. 'Uh, I guess I don't have to share it.' He pulled a slight face as he put his phone away.

Ginny knew if she wasn't so preoccupied with the terrible decision she'd just made, she'd be irked by that tone. Hunter his put his arm around her shoulder. Ginny t uncomfortably, and felt another rumble in her stomach.

'That's okay, we don't have to do it now.' He leaned in and placed a kiss on her cheek.

Her mind flashed with Marcus' eyes, deep and stormy. Guilt rocked her stomach again. Ginny sank like a stone to the floor, heavy and sluggish. She felt small, but w were even smaller, and drew her knees up to her chest. Hunter watched her slip down.

'You okay?'

'...I did something bad,' she whispered at the wall opposite them.

Hunter sat down next to her.

' 'Fess up. What'd you do?' he asked playfully.

Ginny looked at him, took in his warm expression, and looked away.

'Yeah, what'd you do?'

143

Ginny and Hunter looked up at the source of the cold voice.

Marcus was standing in the doorway, looking pointedly at Ginny. His eyes didn't even flash in Hunter's direction; they bored into Ginny in a constant, painful drone.

at Ginny and back at Marcus.

The silence between them lengthened, as Ginny found herself without an excuse or even the words to fabricate one.

But Marcus nodded slowly at her, as if he understood what had just transpired.

'Gotcha. Happy birthday, Ginny.'

He turned, and his head tipped back as he did so, eyes rolling back in his head.

Now Ginny really did feel sick. She lurched up, rushed past Marcus and flew into the bathroom, just barely making it to the toilet bowl to dispose of the contents of second retch, some hands pulled back the hair that was falling around her face, and pinched it at the nape of her neck while she vomited. Her eyes watered from d she finally stopped and was able to relax against the cold tile. She wiped her mouth with a shaking hand.

Someone put their arms around her. She glanced up.

Hunter.

Not Marcus.

'I need a drink,' she choked out, and rose to her feet unsteadily. She moved into the washroom and stuck her mouth under the faucet to rinse out the taste of bile-Hunter followed her awkwardly.

'I'll get you some cold water,' Hunter offered.

'No,' Ginny burbled through a stream of water. She wiped her mouth and began to vigorously wash her hands. She looked back up at Hunter with resolved eyes. 'Al it.'

Ginny no longer wanted to even remember her birthday.

Hunter's eyebrows rose, but he woodenly turned around and went downstairs as Ginny took the liberty of borrowing a spare toothbrush under the sink. She paused toothbrush pack back, remembering the last time she'd used an emergency toothbrush in this house. Memories of Marcus and sweet private moments rushed throu warm and wonderful. Ginny avoided eye contact with her reflection as she scrubbed away the last of the sick taste.

But as she rinsed her mouth again, hot tears sprung from her eyes. She looked at the pathetic excuse of a person in the mirror, crying feebly. Ugh. Marcus deserve gripped the toothbrush and walked to Marcus' room, an apology halfway out her lips.

But the room was empty.

She rushed over to his window and pulled it open. She glanced down into the bushes below. Was his skateboard there? It was impossible to see in the dark.

Ginny looked back out to the hallway, and knew Hunter would be back shortly with drinks for her. Nevertheless, Ginny put the toothbrush in her mouth for some rea herself out the window as carefully as a tipsy person can. She rummaged in the bushes, but found no skateboard.

He'd left.

Ginny began to run, toothbrush in hand.

o

o - o

o - o - o

o - o

o

She found him in the park, at the bench where they'd shared a joint together for the first time. Where Ginny had first realised the gentle but strong undercurrent o love.

She found him broken and small, with his torso bent over his knees and skateboard under his feet, gently rolling from left to right.

Ginny had never really had the power the hurt anyone before.

She stood there a moment, coming to terms with the pain she had caused another human being who did not deserve it. It was a deeply uncomfortable sensation; s mind actively trying to step away from it, to dodge responsibility.

'Hey.' She cringed internally. " Hey – ugh."

'I was ignoring you,' Marcus said simply.

'Oh.'

'You run quite heavily, for someone so small,' Marcus huffed. 'Heard you coming from way back.'

Ginny tucked her hair, which was beginning to frizz up from sweat, behind her ear awkwardly.

'Oh,' she said again.

Marcus climbed to his feet and kicked his skateboard into his hands.

'You also kiss a lot of other people, for someone who says she loves me.'

' A lot of people? I kissed one!' Ginny defended, stung.

'Yeah, that's too many.' He strode away, tossing his board out in front of him and deftly jumping on.

Ginny walked after him.

'Marcus, please!'

'Take a hint, neighbor.'

Ginny stopped in her tracks. With a cry of frustration, she threw the toothbrush still in her hand at his retreating back, but missed by a mile. It landed several feet She saw him glance down at it.

'Did you just throw a toothbrush at me?' He turned his head over his shoulder to look back at her, the ghost of amusement on his face.

'Yes,' she said in defeat.

Marcus gently turned the skateboard back in Ginny's direction, bending down to scoop up the toothbrush as he passed.

'Of all things to throw at me, that's probably in the top ten list of things to make me turn around.' He stopped a few feet in front of her, and threw the toothbrush d her. It hit Ginny in the shoulder. 'I have much better aim than you, though.'

They stared at each other for a moment, Marcus with visible caution.

'I'm sorry.'

'Oh, don't be sorry, it's probably just a result of years of sexist teachers not thinking women are as good at sports as men, so you never got to have the toothbrush lesson.'

'Don't be cute.'

'I'm not, I'm being irreverent.'

Ginny sighed and tipped her head to the side. Marcus almost smiled, but his eyes were hard.

'I'm sorry I threw a toothbrush at you.' Ginny took a deep breath. 'And I'm sorry I kissed Hunter.'

'I am also sorry I threw a toothbrush at you and that you kissed Hunter.'

Ginny fought the urge to give him a stern look, but focused instead on the toothbrush on the ground. She picked it up.

'I love you,' she said earnestly, looking back up at Marcus, whose lips hardened into a smooth line. 'But there was a moment there...where I was tempted by how e to be with Hunter.'

148

She hesitated as Marcus' face stiffened even further.

'Hunter is not someone I really connect with,' she continued, flicking the bristles on the toothbrush absently. 'Hunter asked me to be his girlfriend tonight and he sa about how much he liked me.'

Ginny's mouth twitched at the brief moment of disgust that flickered across Marcus' face.

'It would just be easy and uncomplicated...Hunter is a part of my friend group, and Max actively wanted me to date him – it was kind of weird, really, like it was im pushy. Anyway, he represents everything that I've wanted in a way...just a normal life, a normal boyfriend.' She exhaled forcefully in frustration and continued.

'And even though I know that I love you... I still let him kiss me.'

Marcus blinked and looked to the side.

'And that was really, really shitty of me. And I'm so sorry that I hurt you. And I just want you to know that it had nothing to do you. It was just me.'

She looked back down at the toothbrush in her hand, remembering leaving her mother's house in a storm as her surprise-aunt turned up and flipped her life upside to the welcoming and warm arms of Marcus and his remarkably normal, bar Max, family.

'I don't even know why I did it,' she went on. 'I mean, I know why, but I don't know why why– if that makes sense. And the thing with us, um, with you and the –

what happened.' The confusing sensation of Marcus surprisingly going down on her and the face of her dead step-father coming to mind rattled her again. 'I think..

149

something is wrong with me...?'

Tears pricked her eyes and she looked back up at Marcus, as the odd truth of that sentence sank into her bones. Marcus swallowed, but didn't say anything.

'Anyway, that's what I came here to say. I'm sorry, and it won't happen again...if you...if you still...'

The weight of Marcus' silence and the stillness of his expression ripped her guts down.

Something closed inside Ginny. The door, perhaps, between her and Marcus. That golden connection that brought them together, that intangible string. It closed no dark to her.

It was all dark. And it was because of her.

'I'll let you be alone now.'

She turned away and began the walk back to the party, forcing her shoulders to be still as she did her best to smoothly breathe out sobs and hide any sign of her d dug a fingernail into her palm, the familiar sensation of sharp pain bringing minute relief, but thought desperately of the lighter on her desk at home.

'Ginny?' Marcus called out.

Ginny surreptitiously wiped her tears and made a point of turning around not-too-quickly.

'I'll talk to you tomorrow,' he said. Not cold, not warm. Neutral. Impeccably neutral.

Ginny's mind ran amok with the inferences of his tone.

'...We're okay,' he added after some time. He nodded at her, saluted, and then skated away.

Ginny continued on her path back to the Baker's home and let relieved sobs shake her chest. Somehow, she hadn't ruined everything.

The door to Marcus was open again, a sliver of golden light falling across Ginny.

o

o - o

o - o - o

o - o

o

Ginny turned the corner on Bradley St to see red and blue flashing lights. She stared in surprise as police cruisers drove by with her friends in the back seats. She c eye as they passed, his expression unreadable. She ran home.

Ginny slowed as she walked on her front lawn, becoming more aware of the sound of her mother yelling from inside the house.

'What do you MEAN Ginny isn't there?'

'All the kids were put in the police cars, she wasn't one of them.'

Paul's voice.

Ginny wished she was tall enough to be able to climb back to her room using Marcus' route. Instead she started to creep around the back, just as the front door bu

'Virginia Miller!' Georgia yelled out, striding across the street, as if Ginny would hear her from inside the Baker's house. Paul quickly followed. She swept up the Bak rapped on their door like a jackhammer. 'Ginny!'

'Georgia, come on,' Paul pleaded. 'The neighbors!'

Georgia began to step back and survey the Baker house. To Ginny's surprise, Georgia suddenly began to scale the wall just like Marcus did.

'Georgia, you can't climb peoples' houses!'

'The hell I can't. Ginny!'

Georgia was nearing Marcus' window.

'Mom!' Ginny yelled, and then waved awkwardly under the fierce look her mother threw at her from her precarious position. Ginny had no doubt Georgia would hav the way inside.

Georgia dropped down and practically flew over to Ginny. Ginny flattened her expression, steeling herself for the next bout of distress the night would bring.

'So, this is the thanks I get?'' Georgia yelled.

'Thank you,' Ginny said sarcastically. 'I had a great party.'

'Listen here, you little lunatic. I am responsible for all your friends when they're under my roof. You can't sneak out and lie to me, and

152

then not tell me where you'r She gestured at the house behind her and continued before Ginny could say anything. Ginny noticed a confused-looking Maxine standing in the doorway, watching t match, ensconced in the warm glow of her house. Ginny didn't have time to wonder why she wasn't in the back of a police cruiser.

'I call the cops to break up your little soiree,' Georgia continued, 'and you're not even there.'

'You called the cops on me?' Ginny asked. Something about this irked her, and the increasingly familiar sensation of a rift growing between herself and her mother d

'Well, that's what you get when you lie to me.'

'Okay, okay, you are like – you are like the grand poobah of lies, okay? Y – You're like a lie pro.'

'You ever think that maybe my secrets are to protect you? To keep you happy and safe?'

The issue with Georgia's phone call clunked into place, and it was absurd, so ludicrous that Ginny felt strangely outside her body again for the second time that nigh moment. But the anger of her realisation pulled her back in - back to her body with dark skin. Her body so unlike Georgia's.

'Protect me? You think calling the cops on me is protection?'

'I'll do what I must to teach you a lesson, jerkface.'

'Like sic the cops on YOUR BLACK DAUGHTER? You want me to get shot or something?'

Georgia blinked, and stammered. Ginny seized on that rare moment of weakness.

'Yeah, didn't think about that, did you? This isn't about my safety, or my happiness, this is about you.' Ginny stalked forward, so angry she was almost frothing at t wanted to do this for my birthday and didn't even ASK what I wanted. I go and do the thing that I actually wanted, am a grand total of about 40 feet away from yo the fucking cops on me, under the guise of protection, regardless of what that might actually mean for me. Step up for your Mom of the Year award.'

Georgia actually took a small step backward from Ginny and her fury, but Ginny stepped up and brought her face inches from her mother's.

'You risked my life tonight,' Ginny said through clenched teeth so only Georgia could hear, her voice strange and cold. She allowed Georgia a brief moment, and Gin satisfied to see tears brimming in her mother's eyes. But her mother's beautiful face had transformed to Ginny; it was now cold and ugly. Calculating and petty. Gin this woman anymore.

Ginny marched away from her and straight into the open door Max beckoned her through, not even sparing a glance back at Georgia or Paul. Max closed the door b tears in her own eyes and followed Ginny into the kitchen. Ginny stared at her best friend, her lips trembling.

'Why – why didn't you get taken away like everyone else?' Ginny asked to break the silence, clearing her throat.

'I didn't drink...not after Halloween.'

Max held her hands helplessly in front of her, looking torn between giving Ginny space and reaching out to comfort her.

154

Ginny nodded, and blinked away a few fresh tears, conscious of the fact that Max had never seen her quite like this. Max, whose eyes were already much like a pup day, were even more so right now as she stared at her friend, frozen with sympathy.

'I don't think I have a crush on Georgia anymore,' Max said with a thick voice.

And with that little crumb of validation, Ginny broke, grieving that she lived in a world where her mother chose to be vindictive and reckless directly against her dau a brief moment of passion...she could eventually look past. But this...

Ginny was miserable, and a right state crying in the Baker's kitchen.

'I miss my dad,' she sobbed, and put a hand over her mouth to stifle the noise.

'Aw, honey,' Max said, pulling Ginny in for a hug.

'Why is she like this?' Ginny's voice muffled in Max's shoulder.

'I don't know.' Max patted Ginny's hair, and then pulled back, placing her palms on Ginny's wet cheeks. 'Let's get you to bed.'

Max put her arm around Ginny and led her upstairs.

'God, who knew such a bitch could have such a bod?' Max pondered.

'Max, please.'

'My bad.'

They entered Max's room and Ginny flopped face first in the bed. Max gasped.

'I have an amazing idea,' Max said.

'Mm?'

'You should move in!'

Ginny rolled on one side to look at Max.

'That's very sweet, but I don't think I can. After tonight, I'll have to go – ' Ginny got stuck before the word 'home' could leave her lips. '...back.'

'...Is she always like that?' Max asked quietly. Ginny shook her head.

'No...sometimes she's...almost normal.' Ginny took a deep breath and looked at Max, that cold truth coming over her for the second time that night. 'I don't think it though. I think...there's something wrong with me.'

Max didn't joke. She looked back at Ginny solemnly.

'I don't think there's anything wrong with you. You know I think you're awesome. You're the best thing that's happened to this town in years.'

Ginny closed her eyes, and readied herself to lose her best friend.

'I kissed Hunter tonight.'

'What?!'

'I'm sorry. That's why I was missing, I went running after Marcus to apologise.'

'But why? How could you do that to Marcus?'

'That's what's wrong with me. I love Marcus – sorry – ' she added as Max pulled a 'bleurgh' face, ' and I still did that because Marcus and I had a fight? And I just w wanted, and for everything to be easy. And I wanted it so bad...it felt like I was going to explode.'

'Well, that was a real dick move. You didn't just hurt my brother, you hurt my friend too!' Max yelled.

'I'm sorry...'

Max huffed.

'Let's just go to sleep or whatever.'

Ginny stared in surprise.

'Look, I reserve the right to be really mad at you tomorrow, okay? But I'm not a total dick; you've had a sucky birthday and your mom is – ' Max widened her eyes head as she failed to come up with a word for Georgia. 'And...you're sorry...and you did a whole romantic-comedy run-after-your-love-at-the-airport thing.'

'Thank you...'

Ginny and Max quietly went to bed, with Max pulling up a movie on her phone for them to fall asleep to.

'Loser, I'm home! Thank god your friends are gone.' Marcus called out, knocking on Max's door frame as he went past.

'Whatever, don't careeee. Also Ginny's here.'

'What? Why?' Marcus' voice grew louder as he backtracked.

'Because Georgia is a racist.'

Marcus peered inside the door, and locked eyes with Ginny.

'Your mom's racist?'

'Maybe not racist, but definitely something,' Ginny sighed. 'It's okay, we can talk tomorrow like you said. Just because something shitty happened to me doesn't me get over me doing something shitty to you.'

'You're not wrong,' said Marcus off-handly. 'I am however happy to waive that.' He walked over to Ginny's side of the bed and sat on the floor with his knees up. Gi to him and they exchanged sad glances.

'Are you okay?' they both said simultaneously, and then smiled.

With the tension broken, emboldened, Ginny reached out a hand and rested it on his knee. Would he still let her touch him?

'I'm so sorry,' she whispered.

'I know,' he said gently, and he placed his own hand on hers.

There it was again. Safety and warmth, ensconcing Ginny's tired psyche. Ginny had her best friend on her left, and the boy she loved on her right. Was it really bar minutes ago that Ginny had screamed at her mother? And now happiness was pulsing around her, seeping into her from the smooth comfort of Marcus' hand and th Max's body next to hers.

But Ginny was aware of a dark power in her mind, waiting for the next moment where Ginny wasn't happy to pounce and thrash her to the point of burning her own little alarming.

She was lucky; she had done something unforgivable, though it seemed she was going to be forgiven. But she couldn't rely on that happening again. Ginny couldn'

power take her over again.

Ginny's thoughts wandered across the road and upstairs to her bedroom, where a small piece of card listed the phone number of one Dr Darmody.

Chapter 12

Ginny woke up and immediately ran to the Baker's toilet to throw up again. Apparently she didn't get it all up last night.

Marcus walked out his bedroom and chuckled behind her. He sleepily walked over and pulled her hair back with one hand while stifling a yawn with the other.

'Went a bit too hard last night, eh?'

Ginny groaned, and was sick some more.

'Enough that I'm having to do this again, yes.' Her voice echoed strangely in the toilet bowl.

'Again? You threw up last night?'

Ginny frowned, annoyed.

'You know this.' She paused as a dry retch rocked her. 'Why do you think I went running past you into the bathroom last night before you left?'

'I thought you were going to cry.'

'No. I threw up and had to brush my teeth. Hence the toothbrush I threw at you.'

'Oh. ' Marcus took a moment. 'Gross, why would you throw that at me?'

Ginny answered with another wave of vomit.

'Sorry,' she croaked.

'Ugh, want some water or something?'

'No, I never want to drink anything ever again.'

Marcus laughed, and rubbed her back. Ginny relaxed.

'I think it's over,' she sighed. 'Go away, before you smell it.'

'Too late.'

'Ugh,' Ginny moaned, making her way to the washroom and stealing another toothbrush. 'Tell your parents you need more toothbrushes. I keep using them all.'

'Noted,' he said with faux seriousness as Ginny washed out her mouth and furiously scrubbed her teeth. 'Oatmeal?' he added, with the tone of a rhetorical question Ginny raised an eyebrow.

'Oatmeal...' she said back.

'Eggs?'

Ginny looked at him non-plussed, not troubling to hide her frustration. She did not have the energy for random food riddles.

'Hangover foods,' he said simply, grinning at her.

'Oh.'

Marcus smiled far too happily for Ginny's taste at that particular moment.

'Leave,' she said quietly, waving Marcus away with her hand. 'I'm borrowing a towel. Which is Max's?'

Marcus pointed at a bright orange towel and took his leave. Ginny treated herself to a warm shower and got back out feeling distinctly more human. Max was still s Ginny went downstairs.

'I went with oatmeal,' Marcus said from the kitchen table. 'I really only know how to fry eggs, and I wasn't sure you could handle the oil.'

Marcus handed her a warm bowl of oatmeal, with a drizzle of honey in the shape of a smiley face on top. Ginny looked at Marcus tiredly.

'Are you a morning person or something?'

'Sometimes,' he shrugged as Ginny took the bowl. ' You're welcome.'

'Thank you,' Ginny added, taking a tentative bite of oatmeal. She did not immediately reject it, and took a little more. 'This is good,' she told Marcus.

'Yes, my years of culinary training really paid off. I can microwave milk and oats. But the stirring – ' he pointed at Ginny with the air of a seasoned professional, 'is the wheat from the chaff.'

'I'm too hungover for sarcasm.'

'Aw.'

Marcus put a hand on Ginny's thigh and turned back to his phone that was sitting on the table, scrolling aimlessly. Ginny smiled at the gesture, and enjoyed the wa soothed her sore throat. It had been a good choice.

Someone knocked on the front door. Ginny tensed, recognising her mother's knock.

'Ginny?' came Georgia's voice from the other side of the front door. It was hesitant.

Good.

Marcus turned to Ginny and pulled a questioning face at her.

Ginny shook her head, and Marcus nodded, turning back to his phone as if he hadn't heard Georgia at all.

'Peach, please. I didn't mean it.'

Ginny roller her eyes at the table and stirred her oatmeal.

'Peach? Are you there, baby?'

'Nope,' Ginny muttered quietly.

'What'd she do?' Marcus whispered.

'She called the cops on the party because she was angry I snuck out.'

Ginny pursed her lips. Exhausted from the events of last night, Ginny was feeling a little more lenient on her mom. Everybody makes mistakes. Everybody does rec stupid things. Like kiss boys that aren't their quasi-boyfriend. But Ginny wasn't going to move a muscle until she got a damn apology.

'Shit, I'm sorry.' Marcus looked astounded. 'Damn, you mom is racist.'

'I don't think she actually meant it like that...' Ginny said. 'She didn't even seem to realise. I kinda had to point it out.'

'Don't do that,' Marcus said gently.

'What?'

'Make excuses for her.'

'I'm not. I'm so angry at her...I just don't think she thought about it that way.'

'Ginny, your mom knows what you look like. She knows you look black.'

Ginny blanched at his blunt phrasing.

'Sorry,' he added, seeing her recoil. 'I just – look, I don't wanna fight your battles for you. But don't let her pretend that she doesn't know her daughter's black.' He it was so simple.

Ginny stared back at Marcus.

He kind of had a point.

Ginny tried to find that fire inside her that blazed at Georgia last night, so offended and furious. But the fire was smouldering embers at this point. It lacked energy nap?

'Ginny, baby? I'm sorry, you know I would never do anything to hurt you,' Georgia wheedled from outside.

Ginny's embers set ablaze, and she dropped the spoon into her oatmeal with force, standing up from the table abruptly. Screw apologies. Wide-eyed, Marcus watch Ginny stormed up to the front door and wrenched it open.

'Oh, really?' she challenged. 'What about when you slapped me?'

Ginny almost lost the wind in her sails as she saw that Georgia looked terrible – by Georgia's standards, at least. There were deep, grey bags under Georgia's eyes messy and pulled into a sloppy bun. The perfect face of make-up she drew on every day was gone; that Georgia veneer of intimidating perfection was missing.

In its place, just a small woman, who looked defeated.

Ginny set her jaw to hide her surprise, and narrowed her eyes at her mother. How long had it been since even Ginny had seen this side of her mom?

'Peach,' Georgia started. 'I – I feel awful.'

Ginny folded her arms across her chest.

'I just – you made me so mad when you snuck out like that.'

'Oh, so it's my fault?'

'Well, you shouldn't have left, at least that much is true.'

'Fine! Punish me for leaving! I don't care! That's not the part of last night that I'm really concerned about, believe it or not.'

'I know...that I made a mistake. Okay, I'm human, peach. Okay, your mother is just a regular human!' Georgia's voice began to escalate, and the tiredness on her transformed into a weary determination. 'M – maybe I'm not a perfect mother, I'm no Ellen Baker, but I throw you nice parties and I chaperone your school events!

both hands out to emphasise her speech. 'I've done well for myself and for you and Austin. And you don't seem to appreciate it very much. You were the grumpiest ever seen, and you were rude to Paul – '

'What does this have to do with you calling the cops?' Ginny interrupted.

'Ah, at least you don't deny it. The last few weeks have been tough, I know. But you're not exactly easy to live with sometimes, Virginia.'

Ginny couldn't help but derisively snort.

'And you are?'

'Ohh!' Georgia cried out in frustration. 'Just – come home – please. So we can discuss this in private.'

'No,' Ginny said simply, trying to enjoy the annoyance on her mom's face.

Georgia's eyebrows steepened in warning.

'You know, it's almost funny how angry you are now compared to how contrite you seemed when I opened the door,' Ginny said, with a display of nonchalance.

Georgia inhaled deeply through her nose, eyes closed, acting like it cost her a great deal of patience. Ginny took the moment to quietly take a deep breath as well –

as fun as she had hoped when she pulled the door open.

'Ginny, you left the house without my permission. I let you stay out last night.'

Let? Ginny began to think her 'screw apologies' sentiment was unfounded. Was Georgia really not going to properly apologise – because she didn't truly think she n Ginny could only maintain an

166

unbothered facade for so long, running off the fumes of petering-out rage.

'But you come home now, or you're grounded.'

'Oh, "grounded"? That's okay actually; I'd rather be grounded than dead,' Ginny spat with venom.

Georgia scoffed.

'God, you are dramatic, peach.'

'How do you think Dad might feel about your phone call, huh?' Ginny's voice cracked ever so slightly and the smallest of tears began to bud in her eyes. She cleare she would not show weakness. 'Do you think he might have a slightly different perspective on it?'

Georgia visibly swallowed, but was ready to launch a rebuttal when Marcus sidled up beside Ginny.

'Ms Miller, I think you should go.'

His calm voice was strangely authoritative and his closed expression offered no invitation for response, but Georgia balked.

'This is my daughter I'm trying to talk to, and I will not be told to go by some floppy-haired teenager who hides his pot in a box labelled "math homework".'

Marcus laughed, and Ginny almost believed that he genuinely thought that was funny, if not for a tightening in his eyes.

'Alright, then I'll call the cops,' Marcus said lightly. He rested his hand on the frame of the door, eyebrows raised politely and expectantly at Georgia in the most rem of quiet smugness. He nodded in the direction of Ginny's house. Now that he did seem to find funny, and he barely concealed his smirk.

Georgia stared back at him, sifting for any truth in his words amongst the cruel irony. She huffed, casting her eyes back on Ginny.

'You better be home today.'

'Fine,' Ginny muttered, and shut the door forcefully in Georgia's face.

Ginny and Marcus waited silently until the sound of Georgia's feet faded away. Ginny turned to face him.

'You hid your weed in a box labelled "math homework"?'

'Decoy weed,' he said simply, but he looked seriously at Ginny. 'You okay?'

'She didn't apologise,' Ginny said disbelievingly.

'Yeah...are you okay?' he asked again.

Ginny put her face into Marcus' chest as a response, and allowed him to wrap her in his arms. Ginny let that sensation of safety envelop her and relaxed into the wa shared with her, the gentle way he held her, and the way she squeezed him back – small traces of the deep love they shared for another. Ginny's heart fluttered. Sh aware of how close she had come to losing all of that last night, and gripped him tighter.

Marcus kissed the top of her head, and Ginny looked up at him and wouldn't have been surprised if there were stars in her eyes as she overflowed with appreciation gazed around her face, and one hand came up to brush a stray lock of hair back from her face.

A disgusting noise came from the kitchen entrance. They both looked over, and saw Max pointedly miming sticking her finger in her mouth and making vomit noises had suitably disturbed them, she pulled an overly pleasant face at them, her eyes almost disappearing into the faux-smile and her mouth twisting unnaturally. Her rapidly grew serious.

'Stop being a hallmark movie around me.'

o

o - o

o - o - o

o - o

o

When Ginny arrived at school the following Monday, she was deeply ready for the reprieve from her mom. Ginny had returned for dinner on Sunday, and hadn't utte word to her mother – but Georgia's sour presence had been constant and all-consuming. Ginny had wordlessly accepted her dinner with a snatch, met with Georgia then struck up a conversation with Austin, pointedly falling silent whenever her mom tried to direct any pleasantry towards her. It was awkward, but it was working morning she hugged Austin goodbye, left with a packed lunch and a stiff middle finger directed at Georgia as she waltzed out the door.

Ginny felt a little bit like a loose cannon.

As Ginny got closer to her locker, she started needing to sidle awkwardly between a throng of giggling and heated whispers. As

Ginny pushed past, it became clear Ginny's locker had been spray painted.

S

L

U

T

The angry red word was still shiny. As Ginny stared, a bead of paint rolled down. This was very new, and the culprit was probably nearby. The laughter of the crowd they realised the target of the word was there and reading it. Ginny looked around, her cheeks burning, the crowd merging into a horrific blur of wide smiles. Ginny her locker and placed her palm flat against the top of the 'S' and dragged her hand firmly down, smearing the fresh paint. It worked somewhat. But the word SLUT

made out from where the paint had partially dried underneath the top layer, now surrounded by a wash of thinner paint.

As Ginny turned to leave, she clapped eyes on Hunter, who was standing towards the back of the crowd. His face seemed carved in stone, as he gazed coolly back a Ginny strode forward to meet him.

'What are you angry at me for?' he asked coldly.

It happened before Ginny fully processed the intent that flashed across her mind.

Smack.

Hunter's cheek now had a clear imprint of Ginny's hand painted on his face. The crowd around them gasped and grew silent. Ginny became aware of several phone their direction.

' I didn't do it,' he snapped, as he touched his cheek. He examined the paint transfer on his finger. 'Although maybe you've got a guilty conscience. Where were you of us were being rounded up by police?'

His tone was very pointed, and then his eyes slid to look at something behind Ginny. Ginny turned slightly and saw Marcus making his way up behind her, seeming commotion. She turned back silently, and sheepishly. Hunter glared at her.

'Exactly. So don't slap me – because this is on you.'

Hunter walked past her, and the oof she heard told her he'd intentionally bumped into Marcus as he went. Their audience began to whisper again, the chittering gra nerves like the many voices of a sea of rodents, and the winking of many cameras like their glittering eyes. She stared at the remaining paint on her hand.

'Hey, show's over,' Marcus called out. He shooed them along like cattle. 'You don't have to go home, but you can't stay here,' he intoned sarcastically.

Slowly, people walked away.

Marcus took in Ginny's locker.

'Your first high school reputation. Aw.'

Ginny glared at him. He put his hands up defensively.

'Hey, I didn't paint it. I only just got here.'

171

'I better wash this off,' Ginny said, holding out her hand. 'I'm okay, you can go to your class or whatever.'

Ginny turned and hurried into the next bathroom, ignoring the immediate silence of a couple of girls who were standing there, having clearly been talking about the spectacle, and rinsed off the paint as best she could. The girls exited quickly, leaving Ginny alone. Ginny stared at the red water draining down the sink and the sm that had splashed up onto her wrist. Ginny took a deep breath as her body began to tremble.

She was not okay.

It was happening, what she'd feared as her feelings grew for Marcus, knowing this would place her at odds with her group. She was down at least one friend, she w was suddenly desperate for her lighter. Which was at home.

Ginny picked up her bag and put it on the sink, opening the pockets and rifling through the contents quickly. Keys? No. Tweezers, for eyebrow emergencies? No.

Ginny tipped the bag upside down, looking for something – anything – sharp. A small pharmacy tumbled out of her bag – pain pills, bandages, tampons. She pause safety pin fell out from the bottom of the bag. She stuffed everything else back in the bag haphazardly and locked herself in the toilet cubicle. She pulled down her on the toilet lid, hand shaking. She'd never done this.

Slut.

Slut.

She had cheated on Marcus. She'd led Hunter on. Hell, she'd slept with Marcus somewhere in the vicinity of two minutes after he climbed in her window.

Slut. Good for nothing. Reckless. Own mother doesn't love her the way she should. Own father makes an appearance once a year.

She opened the safety pin and dragged it across her left inner thigh. The scratch was light. It wasn't enough. She went back over the faint line she'd left, experime force. She was surprised by how similar the sensation was to burning – the needle did feel like it seared as a glided across her skin, but it was tiny and concentrate blood began to develop on the line, and Ginny went again and again on the same course, deepening the laceration until she had one long, thick line of blood. Ginny gasped with the expended effort, and then hissed as her skin stung.

Ginny pressed her palm to her face as she began to cry and leaned against the cubicle wall for support.

Such a slut.

It hadn't worked.

Ginny brought the pin down against her skin again in a new fury, starting another line. Her blood shone bright and wet on her skin. She dug as deep as she dared, was an unfamiliar aspect to the cutting than there was to burning, Ginny found. Burning was passive – all she needed to do was move the flame to her skin and sta long as she could stand. No force. Easy.

But she was aware of every strain of her muscle and the tautness of her fingers as she hacked away at her skin, choosing to come back over and over.

This was punishing. It didn't concentrate and release her from the pain like fire did, it exonerated her.

This is for hurting Marcus. This is for hurting Hunter. This is for whatever it was about her that made Georgia slap her, and call the police. This is for whatever made her dad's passions, as he travelled around the globe. This is for being such a bitch. This is for being a slut.

Slash. Slash. Slash.

Ginny sobbed as she cut, barely able to see through her tears, and at some point crossed an invisible line where she had done enough to herself. She slowed, her c and her hand with the pin relaxed to her side. Ginny wiped her eyes clear and looked down at her thigh, and frowned.

It didn't look enough? There were a variety of cuts, some minor scratches, some deeper and bleeding strongly. Some criss-crossed, some vertical, some horizontal.

her palm at the top of the scratches and dragged it down like the paint from earlier, smearing more than half the length of her thigh in blood.

She grabbed some toilet paper and dabbed away the blood, sucking in air through her teeth at the tenderness. She realised she'd flicked blood up onto her cream k somewhat. She wiped everything away, put the bandages from her bag over her thigh and gently pulled her pants back on. She tried to wash the blood from her sh but it resisted. She zipped up her jacket instead, and briefly wiped her face with water.

174

She caught her eye in the mirror before she left. It was the same face. No one would know what she had been in here doing.

Ginny cleared her throat, fixed her hair, and went back out. She walked over to berry tree cautiously.

Hunter was there. But so was Max. No Norah, but Brodie, Press, Jordan and Abby were there.

'Hi...' Ginny said quietly.

Everyone turned around. Max, seated on the armchair, looked like a deer caught in headlights. Press scoffed.

'Hi, slut.' He smiled viciously.

Ginny swallowed, and looked to Hunter. Hunter's cheek was a little pink. Ginny couldn't tell if it was the beginning of a bruise, or from vigorously washing off paint.

Brodie stepped in front of him.

'I'm gonna have to ask you to walk away from my boy.' His tone bordered on playful, but there was an unusual note of sincerity.

Ginny peered around Brodie, and Hunter reluctantly met her eyes.

'I should have told you,' Ginny said.

'That you're a slut?' Press said loudly.

A few people passing in the hall looked over. Ginny bit her lip.

'I'm sorry,' Ginny continued, ignoring Press, and the burning eyes of her – hopefully – friends.

'That you're a slut?' Press said again.

Ginny's eyes snapped at him briefly, biting back a retort.

'Shut up, Press,' Jordan said.

Press grinned indulgently. He was enjoying it.

Ginny turned back to Hunter.

'I'm sorry I hit you, and about Marcus. I shouldn't have...'

'You had your chance,' he said quietly. 'I hope you have fun with that loser – because I am a great boyfriend. You knew I liked you, and you had me running you an to your secret therapy appointment, like an idiot. That's real nice, Ginny.'

Ginny blinked, and looked down in embarrassment as the rest of the group looked at her. She had asked him that favour as a friend, but that didn't seem to matter

'Hunter, go easy,' Max said. She glanced at Ginny, unsure what she could say. 'Ginny's going through some stuff right now.'

'What?' Hunter said rhetorically. 'Literally, what – because I don't know what I did to deserve this.'

Hunter stepped around Brodie and stared down at Ginny. Ginny nodded.

'You didn't do anything,' she agreed. 'That's why I'm sorry.'

Ginny glanced around at the faces of her friends. Max looked stuck in the middle and Jordan impassive. But everybody else ranged from mad to outwardly hostile.

'Yeah, and any therapist worth their salt is gonna tell you that your actions have consequences,' Abby said cattily.

'Slut consequences,' Press grinned.

'Oh, shut up, Press!' Ginny exploded. 'You – I don't even know why everybody likes you. You haven't said a single nice thing in the whole time I've known you, so e don't care what you have to say.'

It felt good to say. But Ginny regretted it immediately. The vibe in the group changed immediately, and Ginny knew she had stepped over a line she couldn't come Ginny looked at Max, who was looking down at her knees.

Ginny took a step back, and looked at Hunter again.

'I really am sorry.'

And she left, walking past Hunter as if in slow motion. Ginny would never be allowed back at berry tree again. As she walked, she saw Press out of the corner of he motion, and she turned to face him slightly as she passed. His hand was coming out from his pocket, and there was a rhythmic metallic sound. Ginny didn't have ti before the paint was being sprayed across her. She froze in surprise, and was rooted to the spot as he sloppily painted the word SLUT on the front of her jacket.

' You painted it?' Hunter said.

Max stood up and pushed the paint can out of Press' hand.

'What the hell? That is way too far,' Max yelled. 'What are you gonna do next, write dyke on me?'

'Might be good advertising,' Press sniffed.

177

Ginny hurriedly unzipped her jacket and pulled it off. She folded her arm across the front of her shirt, trying to cover up as much of the blood stain as she could wit She glanced around at everyone's eyes – most everyone was looking at Press, but Hunter was looking at Ginny's midriff and then his eyes met hers in alarm.

Ginny backed away, and then began to run.

'Ginny!' Max called out.

But Ginny didn't turn around. She ditched her jacket in the nearest bin and ran the whole way home, her breath painful and laboured. She didn't even stop to close behind her as she arrived home, and sprinted up the stairs. With tears in her eyes, she snapped up Dr Darmody's card and dialled.

Chapter 13

Dr Darmody smiled politely at Ginny, who shifted uncomfortably and fiddled with her fingers. In a stroke of luck, Dr Darmody had a cancellation that day, and the handful of clients on the wait-list hadn't responded. A wardrobe change and a short ride-share later, and Ginny was plopping onto Dr couch, squaring off against him while he prepared a notepad.

'So, Ginny,' he began. 'How are you?'

'Good,' Ginny replied automatically. 'You?'

'I'm good.' He tilted his head a little as he looked at her. 'What can I do for you?' he prompted.

'...I don't know,' Ginny said honestly.

Dr Darmody smiled.

'Well, let's start with what prompted your call today, and general concerns. And then we can try discuss goals – what you want to get out of therapy.'

Seemed simple enough. Ginny opened her mouth, but paused, not sure how to start. And not sure how to open up to a complete stranger.

'I think,' Ginny said, taking a deep breath, and continuing uncertainly, 'that I'm having more trouble than I should be.'

'Okay. In what way?'

A series of images flashed in Ginny's mind: Georgia slapping her, Paul at the dinner table, blood on her thigh, her Dad riding away on a motorcycle, Hunter's impass rolled past in a police cruiser.

'Um.'

The extent of issues coming to her mind seemed so excessive that Ginny laughed.

'How much time you got?' she joked.

'Just under an hour,' Dr Darmody quipped back with a grin, making an exaggerated glance at his watch.

Ginny smiled back, but then her face fell as she grew serious.

'I hurt myself,' she said bluntly. She blinked uncomfortably, uttering this fact for the first time ever to another person. But Dr Darmody showed no reaction, other th encouragement. 'Sometimes...I get these feelings. Like they're gonna explode out of my – my eyes...my teeth...'

Dr Darmody made a brief note, his pen scratching.

'And then I burn myself. It concentrates it, like a release. And then I feel better. But today it changed. I – I cut myself, and I kind of...punished myself.'

Another pen scratch – slightly longer.

'Why did it change, do you think? Did something trigger it?'

Ginny pursed her lips.

'Just some friend drama at school. And I wanted to burn myself, but my lighter was at home. I found a safety pin...' Ginny trailed off, her cheeks growing hot with t shame, and remembering the viciousness she'd attacked her own skin with.

It suddenly felt very weak to have cut herself, like a fundamental flaw in her person.

'How long have you been self-harming for?'

Ginny looked off to the side as she cast her mind back, and then frowned.

'Er, like 4 years or so?'

Dr Darmody's eyebrows tweaked ever so slightly.

'You're 16, yes?'

'Yeah...turned 16 just the other day'

'Okay. Do you remember what happened the first time?'

Ginny's face stilled.

...

Ginny was 11, and absolutely delighted that her father Zion was staying with her mom and Austin in between trips. Mom wouldn't accept Ginny's grandparents offe stipend for Dad's contribution to the bills. Barely making ends meet as it was, there was less food on the table, but more smiles and infinite hugs with her dad, the was too big for Magic Carpet Ride, but not too big for piggy backs. Mom sang in the kitchen loudly to the radio. Ginny had grown-up big-sister time with Austin whi squirrelled themselves away in mom's bedroom. Ginny was riding the motorbike on her dad's lap slowly up and down the street, then by herself with Dad running a whooping and yelling encouragement. Laughing so hard her stomach hurt, splayed out on the apartment floor. It had been a paradise, cherishing their undoubtedly before Dad went off on his next adventure that he couldn't bring Ginny on, waiting for the next time Ginny could accompany him .

Mom and Dad were arguing again. Raised voices. Ginny was hiding with Austin in his bed at the sound of hands smacking on bench-tops and doors slamming. Mom set in a hard line as she washed dishes, resolutely not looking behind her as Dad pulled his things together. "I'm sorry, gummy bear" whispered to her one night, w gentle hand brushing through her hair, and then Dad retreated out the door and off on his motorbike, the rear light sliding away while Ginny clutched his lighter at road, tears blossoming.

Mom barely uttered a word the entire following week. Ginny was playing with her dad's lighter, missing him, and suddenly had the idea to glance her fingertips thro flames. She was quick to pick a prime location of skin to keep her secret hidden. Ginny quietly sobbed in her room as she lashed her thigh with fire when, two days departure, Mom drank a bottle of wine for early dinner and excused herself for bed by 5pm, leaving Ginny to bathe and feed Austin.

Packing her life into well-used boxes, and staring out the back of the car at the umpteenth "You are now leaving..." town sign, preparing for the next time Mom wou a man.

...

'My parents broke up. Again,' she added resentfully. 'For like the tenth time.'

182

Ginny cleared her throat, which was suddenly stuck. Dr Darmody was looking at her sympathetically. Ginny laughed and sniffled, shaking her head and waving her dismissively. She shrugged.

'Parents don't always stay together, right?'

'No,' Dr Darmody agreed, and went on, 'So, the burning is a coping mechanism for getting through overwhelming feelings.'

'I guess.'

'And what sort of feelings are you struggling with?'

'Um...' Ginny had never really thought about that. 'I guess mostly when I feel sad, or angry. Ashamed.'

'Can you elaborate on that?' Dr Darmody asked in interest.

'I dunno. Like – when someone makes a bit of an issue of the fact that I'm black, but I dressed up as Britney Spears for Halloween.' Ginny threw up frustrated hand people can't dress as Britney Spears. Or maybe we can't? I wouldn't know!'

'Or this guy in my friend group, Press, was like unnecessarily mean when we had a party this one time. I was literally only talking about A Star Is Born and it just m like I can't really be myself, you know?'

Ginny's voice was slowly getting louder.

'Sometimes Dad is meant to visit, and then he cancels because he gets a sudden opportunity that he can't pass up. Or when mom started dating a new guy immed moving to town, when she promised she wouldn't. Or when she wouldn't let Austin come to therapy after stabbing someone. Or when she married Kenny and tried lives into his, and we stopped doing shit like eating pizza. Who doesn't eat pizza?'

'Oh! And there was that time I went on a date with Hunter and she was all weird about it when I got back. And now she doesn't even know that I'm dating Marcus, freaked out when she thought I liked him – " Because I'm her" ,' Ginny mocked with a nasty face and a silly voice. 'Like I'd let myself get pregnant. She forced me o anyway.'

'And don't even get me started on her whole secret identity thing and the slapping thing. I just – want – a normal – mom.'

Ginny folded her arms across her chest stubbornly and leaned back against the couch, sulking. She realised she'd gone off-topic, and sighed angrily.

'I'm picking up on some anger at your mom.'

There was a wry twinkle in Dr Darmody's eye, so Ginny bit back a snarky response.

'Yeah.'

'Do you still think your mom won't come to therapy?'

'No way,' Ginny snorted.

'That's disappointing.'

Dr Darmody appeared to be making some dot points on his note pad.

'Okay, Ginny, so I can tell you based on what you said there alone, we would really need at least ten sessions to make any real kind of progress for you, I feel. So, should try think of some goals, and since your mom's not supporting you, see what we can do payment-wise to make this more accessible – if you're happy to com

'...You won't just...' Ginny shrugged, 'give me some kind of pill to keep my feelings in check?'

'I don't think that would help you. Numbing your feelings won't take away the situations that you're in.'

Ginny chewed on her lip a little, resenting that truth.

'I think that something called cognitive behavioral therapy might help you to assess and manage your emotions, and that's what I would be taking you through. So some goals...'

He looked at Ginny expectantly, who gazed back.

'Um...get my mom to stop being...so much like my mom?'

Dr Darmody looked at Ginny kindly.

'Unfortunately your therapy isn't for other people. You won't learn how to help your mom, but hopefully you'll learn how to help yourself. Try think of something for

'I guess it'd be nice to be less angry.'

'Okay,' said Dr Darmody, and he began to write.

'But everyone's always making me angry,' Ginny continued in confusion. 'How can I make myself less angry without changing other people?'

'I hear what you're saying,' Dr Darmody said gently, 'but you can't control other peoples' actions and feelings. Just your own.'

Ginny began to scowl.

'What, so everybody else just gets to keep doing what they're doing?'

'Yes, essentially,' Dr Darmody said quietly, and he kept eye contact with Ginny. 'Therapy can be about your relationships and any issues you're having within them, the best course of action is to remove yourself from a relationship, but ultimately therapy is about you.'

Ginny blinked and looked away, a lump in her throat.

'What's bothered you about that?' Dr Darmody prodded.

'Uh,' Ginny said thickly. 'Just made me think of a mistake I made.'

'Mm?'

Ginny stared back at him, reticent.

'This is what you're here for,' he reminded her.

'...That guy Marcus, I mentioned? We're together, but I kissed another guy – that guy Hunter,' Ginny sighed, looking down at her knee, not wanting to risk seeing j across his face.

'Okay. What about that do you want to discuss?'

'I guess why I kissed him.'

'Okay.'

Ginny scratched at the fabric on her knee with one finger in silence, and then chanced a look at Dr Darmody. He was waiting politely. Ginny assumed that years wo had made him a master of staring at someone without appearing impatient or rude.

186

'Marcus and I had had a fight,' Ginny relented after some time.

Dr Darmody nodded.

'And I got all weird, like I sometimes do, and I just really wished things were easy. Marcus really gets me. And I get him. But he doesn't fit with my friends, and my like him. And Marcus is...private...and doesn't really care about labels – which is fine, honestly – but Hunter is the complete opposite. And I could just see how easy were with Hunter and not Marcus. And then I kissed him, and almost lost Marcus. Which would have been the worst thing ever.'

'You said you went weird?'

'Yeah,' Ginny said non-plussed, surprised that this was the section he'd focussed on.

'Weird how?'

Ginny exhaled forcefully. This was exhausting; it was remarkably taxing to open up. Ginny was ready for bed, and it was not even midday.

'Sometimes...and I don't know why...but sometimes something will happen, like this thing with me and Marcus,' Ginny skirted, as she would not be recounting that kind of end up out of my body?'

Dr Darmody looked expectant, so Ginny carried on.

'Like, instead of being in my body, I'm in...my mind? It's like I'm a pair of eyeballs and a brain and that's it.' Ginny pulled a face at the visual.

'Hmm,' said Dr Darmody. 'What caused this?'

Damn.

'Uh, my argument with Marcus.'

'What was the argument about?'

Double damn.

'Uh...' Ginny's heartbeat started increasing, and she swallowed uncomfortably, looking away from him. She curled her fingers inward on one hand, and dug her nails

'Ginny...' Dr Darmody said gently. 'Please don't do that to yourself.'

He was looking at her hand. Ginny relaxed her hand in surprise.

'You didn't mention that,' he continued softly. 'So, burning, cutting – which is new, and also pressing your nails into your skin?'

Ginny blinked, and instinctively put her hand under her knee.

'Oh. I didn't...even think about that.'

'Are you okay?'

Ginny nodded.

'Sometimes in therapy we do have to discuss uncomfortable topics. But if you're not ready, or really don't want to, as long as you're not in danger or anything, we d talk about them. If you want to stop, we can stop. I can give you my best recommendation, but you're the boss here.'

Ginny liked that.

A boss. In control. Autonomous.

Something she never was.

'Do you want to try talk about it?'

Ginny's stomach flipped at the thought of having to tell an almost complete stranger about Marcus' head between her thighs, and how that somehow made her thin step-father. They'd already opened a few cans of worms that day – did she need to add another?

'Maybe next time?' she asked.

'That's fine. I feel like we have a lot to unpack, and we are starting to run out of time,' he glanced absently down at his watch. 'So let's nail down these goals. What something regarding your self-harm?'

'...like stopping?'

'Yes.'

Ginny took an oddly strangled breath.

'But if I don't...I don't know what else to do. I do it because everything else hurts, just sitting there and existing. It hurts. It's the only thing that makes it stop.'

'I understand. Self-harm is a coping mechanism. But it's a harmful one. Your goal might be to exchange self-harm with a healthy coping mechanism.'

Dr Darmody then encouraged Ginny to pull out her phone, and explained about a variety of apps she could download to help her get over the urge. Distractions, an He briefly took her through something called 'box breathing'. He handed her worksheets with grids of boxes saying "What triggered the event?", "Feelings/Thoughts be brought back for three events Ginny struggled with for Dr Darmody to discuss on their next visit. He recommended Ginny start a journal and try to log her emot their triggers, to try narrow down what bothered her most. They settled on the one goal for now – getting Ginny to stop hurting herself, and trialling alternative cop

'...So therapy...has homework,' Ginny said dubiously.

Dr Darmody cracked a grin.

'Tragically, yes.'

They then outlined that Ginny would attend every fortnight to start off with, and review later if they needed to increase or decrease their sessions. He offered her a discounted rate that Ginny was able to pay 50% of after she attended, and then the remaining 50% would be direct debited on their off-week. It still wasn't cheap, shifts at Blue Farm Cafe she would just make it.

As Dr Darmody walked Ginny out the door, she thanked him profusely.

Ginny scheduled a ride-share, and resolutely decided to go back to school instead of home. Since therapy was all about getting through things, she figured she'd be through them.

o

o - o

o - o - o

o - o

o

Marcus caught up with Ginny at her locker, which was still red with a fuzzy SLUT written on it, as he travelled between classes.

'You stalking me, neighbor?' Ginny asked nonchalantly, as she put her backpack away, pretending she was not quietly seething again at the paint on her locker.

Marcus ignored her.

'Max said you left school.'

'You leave school all the time.'

'I know I do. But you don't.'

'We did just the other day.'

'Yes, I'm a bad influence. I feel like everybody has warned you of this.'

Ginny and Marcus grinned at each other. Then Marcus glanced at her locker.

'You good?'

Ginny sighed, exhausted from pouring out her soul in Dr Darmody's office.

'I don't wanna talk about it.'

'Okay,' Marcus shrugged. 'You're the boss.'

Ginny hid a smile. She was the boss for the second time that day.

'You're wearing a different shirt,' Marcus commented. 'And you've lost your coat.'

'Very observant,' said Ginny, thankful that Max hadn't passed on everything that happened to Marcus.

'Why?' he asked.

'What is this – an interview?'

Marcus put up a defensive gesture, and then slid his hands gently around Ginny's waist from behind. Ginny paused for a moment, as Marcus rested his chin on her hair tickling her ear. He was warm and solid; Ginny almost instantly relaxed. Marcus turned his mouth towards her ear.

'We've still got five minutes before the next class,' he whispered suggestively, kissing her softly on her neck.

Ginny rolled her eyes.

'Do you want to solidify my new reputation?'

'Ah,' Marcus intoned. 'I did not think of that.'

Ginny pulled out her English books, shut her locker and turned around, Marcus' arms falling away.

'That's because you weren't thinking with that,' and she tapped Marcus' forehead, and he grinned.

'Sure you don't just wanna ditch?'

Ginny gazed at her locker.

SLUT

'Nope. I'm the boss.'

192

'Yeah, you are,' Marcus said, raising his eyebrows, a strange smile on his face.

Marcus gave Ginny a lingering kiss, and then they parted. Ginny walked into English with her head held high, sitting down in her seat next to Max. Hunter was sittin in front of Max, chatting.

They both fell silent when Ginny turned up. Ginny stoically arranged her books, and then pulled out her phone. She opened up a new Note document entitled 'Feelin First entry: Bad-ass.

'Hey, you're back,' said Max.

Ginny looked over with a neutral expression. Max looked borderline weepy, while Hunter was looking at the corner of the desk he was sitting on. Ginny was surprise as soon as Ginny arrived.

'I'm back,' Ginny agreed, keeping her voice intentionally level.

'We didn't think we'd see you again today,' said Hunter.

Ginny looked up at him, but Hunter kept staring at the desk.

'Neither did I,' Ginny said.

'I saved your jacket,' said Max. 'It's probably a goner, but you might as well try to fix it?'

'What about your shirt?' asked Hunter.

Now he made eye contact with Ginny. Ginny stared back, trying to read what Hunter knew or thought he'd seen on her shirt, but was taken aback by the concern in expression and the underlying question – is she okay?

193

'...My shirt's okay...' Ginny said.

Hunter gazed at her for a moment, and then nodded.

'Good.'

Hunter went and sat at his own desk across the way without another word.

'Well, I'm glad you're back,' said Max. 'I know that whole thing is happening with you guys right now, but I am so stressed I have hives in really annoying places. It the thought of volunteering with EDCO – on top of homework, and school, and rehearsal – it's like, it makes me want to chop myself up into hamburger meat. I don handle MANG drama on top of everything.' Max cradled her face in her hands, and pretended to sob.

Ginny blinked. Did Max still want to be her friend? Ginny's heart leapt, and she rushed to respond.

'Shit. You're so scheduled.'

'Not really. Just all the stuff you have to do for college. Which is pointless anyway since a psychology degree will be useless when the planet implodes in 30 years.'

'Stuff you have to do for college?'

'Volunteering in Peru, and winning a mock business proposal competition,' she said sardonically. 'Hunter did that,' she added.

Ginny felt a pinprick of fear, realising that Ginny had precisely nothing to contribute other than her grades.

'What extra-curriculars have you done?' she asked Max.

'Jesus,' Max said, eyes widening at the daunting question. 'Um, flute, French, piano, field hockey, basketball, soccer, tap, ballet, hip-hop, jazz, pottery, karate and t The pinprick grew into a larger sensation of panic in Ginny's chest, and Ginny struggled to respond from the bottom of a hole, lofty education aspirations far, far ab not feel so much like a boss anymore.

Mr Gitten entered, and announced to the class that they would be entering the National Junior Pulitzer Essay Contest – Where Do You Feel You Most Belong. Appare college applications.

Gitten would select one person from their class to be submitted to the regional competition.

Ginny desperately wanted to be that person. She needed to be that person.

Ginny pulled out her phone discreetly and opened up her new Feelings note.

Second entry: Doomed.

o

o - o

o - o - o

o - o

o

Max bolted after class to get to rehearsal for Sing Sing, practically ditching Ginny's jacket, all rolled up in a ball, from her backpack at Ginny as she did. Ginny stuff inside her bag, but slowly packed up her books, weighed down by her complete and utter lack of extra-curriculars. Ginny was never getting into a good college.

Where did she belong?

As if Ginny hadn't been asking herself that her whole life. Tall about a light essay topic. For a moment...she'd hoped it would be Wellsbury...

Ginny noticed Hunter was also slow in packing up his things, standing at his desk but bending over his backpack. Students were filtering out, Mr Gitten overseeing Ginny a little shrewdly. Seeing Hunter remaining as well though, Mr Gitten gave a brief nod and deemed it suitable for him to leave, clearly trusting Hunter with the of ensuring everybody left class. Ginny held back a scoff, not wanting to make her presence known.

Bur once they were alone, Hunter turned to face her.

Ginny stood uncertainly, ready for another verbal lashing. Hunter's face was impassive. After a few moments, Ginny had to look away, and tried to ignore that tickle that told her an urge to burn was locked and loaded, ready to fire. Ginny was the boss.

'Are you actually okay?' Hunter asked eventually, his voice even.

'Yeah,' Ginny said brightly. Perhaps a little too brightly. 'Just a little freaked about the essay – I've just found out I'm the most behind I could possibly be for extra-c Ginny could see Hunter measuring her response. Did he actually know that was blood on her shirt? Or did he just wonder?

'Are you okay?' Ginny asked before Hunter could delve any further into the spatter he'd seen on Ginny's shirt.

Hunter took a moment, his eyes growing shiny.

'You really hurt me,' he said bluntly. 'I don't know if I can be your friend.'

He almost sounded regretful.

Ginny could see the hole in the fabric of her friendships this would tear. Good bye Brodie, Jordan and Press. Well, Press wasn't such a loss. But MANG were part and Max wanted to be her friend still, Ginny couldn't see how that would work.

And truthfully, Ginny would miss Hunter.

Ginny's mind became clouded with a type of tunnel-vision. Her surroundings somewhat disappeared, and she saw Hunter's mouth dropping its fatal blow over and o know if I can be your friend".

Ginny looked down at her feet, almost surprised to see they were still there, as she felt like her legs had been knocked out from underneath her. Ginny dimly regist Feelings note was going to be overworked.

'That's fair,' she whispered. There was nowhere to go – no path around the understanding that this was Ginny's fault. Not seeing a purpose in standing there any lo grabbed her things, cast a hopeless look at Hunter and quietly started to leave.

'Don't – don't you have anything to say?' Hunter said incredulously, standing rigidly at his desk.

Ginny turned back, defeated.

'Is there anything I could say?' she asked rhetorically, and then carried on after Hunter was silent. 'I can't un-kiss you. I can't un-fall in love with Marcus. I can't tak up.'

'What is wrong with you?' Hunter asked, sounding as if he actually wanted an answer.

'That's what I'd like to know,' Ginny remarked glibly.

'Do you like me, or don't you?' Hunter demanded. 'Because I – ' Hunter stopped talking suddenly, and stared at Ginny imploringly.

Ginny took a moment. Hunter's eyes were bright with unshed tears, and Ginny was stabbed with the realisation of what she'd put him through. He looked at a total Ginny had been the one who ripped the rug out from under him.

'I wanted to like you,' Ginny said honestly.

Hunter blinked and looked away sullenly.

'You are a much better fit for me in a lot of ways. But I love Marcus. I tried to tell you, but I didn't. I'm sorry.'

Ginny received an alert on her phone, and glanced at it.

Dad: You loving your first fall in New England?

The foliage is outrageous

Ginny sighed. She was not in the mood for small talk about trees, and she looked back at Hunter. She just wanted the day to end, after a perpetual emotional roller and graffiti. Hunter looked like his jaw had turned to stone. Fatigued, she pulled her bag over her shoulder and turned to leave, actively clamping down thoughts of

'I won't be an option when you realise what he's like, I hope you know that.'

Ginny froze, and exhaled forcefully.

'You know,' she said, turning back around, a little bit of acid seeping into her tone, pinching the bridge of her nose and then flaring her hand out. 'People keep sayin much of a jerk Marcus is – but Press is like your best friend and he's a total and complete dick. So unless you're kicking him out, don't talk to me about Marcus.'

Hunter looked at Ginny sourly.

'Again, I'm sorry about all this,' Ginny said angrily. 'I'm just pissed off now.'

Hunter opened his mouth, but Ginny's phone dinged again.

Dad: It's a little cold though. Glad I packed my jacket

Ginny's internal rollercoaster took a massive up-swing.

He was here.

'I have to go,' she said, sprinting out the class and into the halls.

Ginny ran past berry tree, ignoring the faces of her former-friends as she dashed past, seeing her father Zion Miller sweep gracefully into her school. His eyes caug smiled easily, hands out on his hips, all decked out in bike gear. Nothing could bother her now, all thoughts of burning skin and scorned friends behind her.

Ginny's face split into a wide grin, and happiness ballooned in her chest.

'Dad!'

'Hey!'

She dashed into his opens arms, and was swept up and spun – up, up and away. Ginny was 5 years old again, on Magic Carpet Ride. Every moment in her father's bliss, like gravity itself couldn't touch her. He was here.

Ginny was chosen.

Chapters 14

Georgia was wearing a sundress, smiling enticingly from the upstairs balcony of their home, despite the nippy air and overcast day.

'Hey. Thanks for the fence,' she called down at Zion as her way of greeting, as he lumbered up the yard with Austin on his shoulder.

Ginny struggled not to roll her eyes as her dad's low voice rumbled smoothly back.

'Hey, peach.'

Her parents always sounded like they were two seconds away from going at it – whether this was romantically speaking or an all-out argument – and Ginny hated i dangerous to each other; never having their guard up. Georgia and Zion only ever ended in pain.

Ginny glanced back at Marcus across the street who was just disappearing into his house after being introduced to her dad, before looking back at her mom. Georg fixated on Zion's form. Ginny scowled at Georgia, who met her look only after Zion walked past the threshold.

'What?' Georgia challenged after a beat. 'Are you actually going to speak to me? But your impression of a mime is coming along so great.'

Ginny shook her head and headed up to her room, footsteps heavy as she considered navigating between her mother and her father. She hid her jacket, painted wi slut,in the bottom of her closet to be addressed at another time and then stood with her hands on her hips, chewing her lip.

Spending time with her dad would mean spending time with her mom.

She huffed and went back downstairs where Zion, seated on the couch with Austin, was presenting him with a small gift. Georgia observed opposite with a glass of angelic expression.

Ginny hesitated in the doorway, making eye contact with Georgia, whose eyebrows rose in unspoken challenge.

'There you are, gummy bear. Sherpa Ang Tharkay's memoir.'

He held a book out in Ginny's direction. Georgia's perfect eyebrows tweaked ever so slightly, waiting to see what Ginny would do as the book hung in the uncomfor Ignoring Georgia, Ginny strode in and gratefully took the book from her dad.

'One of the most famous Mount Everest guides. Riveting read.'

Ginny flipped it open to a random page.

'Some of the words are underlined. Is it a code?' she asked.

'No,' Zion said simply, discreetly winking at her. Ginny grinned.

If joy had a physical state, Ginny decided it would be liquid. An effervescent, golden liquid with the radiance of sunshine that bubbled up inside, as it did now when warmly at her.

She wanted more.

But Georgia was peering at her over her wine glass with a glower that then swept away for a beautiful smile as Zion glanced between the two of them.

'Thanks, dad,' Ginny said, not troubling to hide a resentful glare at her mother. 'I'm gonna go read it.' She turned on her heel.

'What's that about?' she heard Zion ask as she left.

'Oh, teenagers,' Georgia said flippantly. 'She's been a little moody recently.'

'Hmm.'

Ginny gritted her teeth, restraining from stomping upstairs, and buried herself in her new book upstairs at her desk away from the eyes of her mother. She took ou started jotting down the underlined words she came across, looking for the pattern, but got lost and began doodling on the page a variety of spirals and jagged line her hand becoming more aggressive and then her pen shredded through the paper.

'Ugh!

She threw her pen down and rested her head on folded hands.

Her father was downstairs, he was here in her life for the first time in months and months. Valuable time. And Ginny couldn't stand being in the same room as her straightened hair was flowing gently over her eyes. She stared at it, and went to stand in front of her mirror restlessly.

Small and petite, even in the regions where Georgia was voluptuous, and dark where Georgia was fair, Ginny really didn't look much like her mother. Except perhaps eyebrows which cut boldly across the faces of both women. Ginny tugged at her unnaturally straight hair and glared at the crumpled mess on her floor that was her knit shirt, her mouth turning down in loathing as a dark hole grew aggressively in the pit of her stomach. It was somehow Georgia. All Georgia. The sleekness of he pumpkin-spice latte that surely came free with that shirt. And where was Ginny?

Her body was there. Those were her brown eyes. She could smile and see her teeth. That was her chest rising and falling in increasing speed as her lungs seemed t boxed in and squeezed from all angles. It was her lips that trembled.

But Ginny wasn't there.

Ginny shuddered and marched into the bathroom. She washed her hair in the shower, gently squeezing the excess water from it afterwards. She took care in apply cream, scrunching it towards her scalp, the locks of her hair falling back into familiar patterns and spirals. She tipped her head towards the floor and diffused her ha weight of excess moisture slowly dry out. It would take hours to dry properly, but Ginny gave the mirror a watery smile as her curls reformed and breathed deeply,

returning to stasis. She dabbed her face with her towel, absorbing a few stray tears.

There was Ginny.

There was a gentle knock on the door. Ginny sighed quietly, drying off the rest of her face and re-arranging her clothes, the damp fabric sticking uncomfortably.

'Yeah?'

'Can I come in?' Zion asked.

'Sure, Dad.'

Zion gently opened the door. He paused partway inside, his eyes raking over Ginny's hair and his gentle smile faded as he fixed Ginny with a concerned look. He lea against the sink.

'Do you wanna tell me what's going on?'

'I'm sure Mom will fill you in,' Ginny remarked in a clipped tone.

'I want to hear it from you,' he said firmly.

Ginny put her towel away and went back to her room, Zion following behind. Ginny sat on her bed and pulled her laptop towards her.

'I have an essay to work on,' she side-stepped, opening up a blank document and making a show of typing.

The clickity-clack of Ginny's determined fingers filled up the space between them.

'Oh, yeah? What essay is that?' Zion towered in the doorway.

Ginny latched onto the different topic.

'AP English. We're writing about where we most belong. It's for a contest.' Ginny grit her teeth as her stomach swooped again with fear of how far behind she was i curriculars.

'And where are you writing about?'

'Good question,' Ginny muttered without looking up, pulling a face, still making an obnoxious amount of noise of her keyboard.

'Hmm, it's interesting that you're typing so much without knowing your topic.'

The clacking stopped and Ginny looked up sheepishly at her dad, caught in the act. Zion grinned at her.

'What's the matter, gummy bear?'

Ginny measured up her father, and the deep love he held for her mother. Ginny knew it was always there; the undercurrent could be felt in the room by any poor by Georgia and Zion looked at each other. It was a love that brought him back periodically despite history showing again and again that it just didn't work between the She wondered where she, his daughter, fell on the scale of his love and then the air turned to ice in her chest.

'It doesn't matter.'

'And why's that?'

'You're not going to be here for too long, I assume,' Ginny hedged. 'It doesn't matter that much, and I'd rather not let it ruin your visit.'

'Is this about those texts you sent?'

'No. You can ignore those, it's fine.' Ginny pulled her phone out from her pocket casually and opened up her Feelings note.

Stuck.

Zion gazed at her for a moment, his expression inscrutable. He then started peering around her room.

'Wow, I see a lot of my work in here,' his eyes flitted across

a variety of his prints. '...Except for that one. That's dope.'

Ginny's face grew hot as Zion walked over to inspect Marcus' birthday present that she had tacked onto the wall.

'Who did it?'

'Uh, a friend for my birthday.' Ginny looked resolutely at her computer and erased her gibberish text. The last thing she needed was to get in another blowout argu Georgia about a boy, and worse a skateboarding pot-smoking boy. She had far more pressing things on her mind.

'Was it that boy across the street? Marcus?'

Ginny blinked.

'Uh, yes, actually. Good guess,' she remarked off-hand.

Zion's eyes burned with unasked questions as Ginny feigned composure.

'Where I most belong...' Ginny mused out loud in a stage whisper.

'It's good,' Zion prompted. 'The texture of it, and your expression. Did you pose for it?'

'No, it was a surprise.'

'Hmm.'

Out of the corner of her eye, Ginny could see Zion smiling beguilingly at her.

The last thing Ginny needed was Georgia finding out about Marcus.

'Wellsbury was a bit of a surprise too,' Ginny said off the cuff.

'Maybe I should write about this place. It's okay.'

'You like it here then?'

His voice was conversational, but Ginny heard it – that note of confusion with just the slightest hint of disbelief.

'I think so,' Ginny shrugged. 'It's probably the best place we've lived so far.'

'Hmm, and what's good about it? What makes it where you most belong?'

She glanced by accident at Marcus' painting.

'Well, I actually have friends here,' she said, and then her face fell.

Had.

She hitched a faux smile on her face.

'So that's a plus.'

'That is a plus,' he conceded. 'How come you straightened your hair?'

'I just washed it out,' Ginny said defensively, a hand going up to her curls.

'Yeah, but why'd you straighten it?'

'I dunno,' Ginny shrugged. 'I – I thought it'd be nice.'

Zion lapsed into silence, and Ginny chanced a look at him; her insides writhed like snakes with insecurity at the almost pitying expression he wore.

'What?'

Zion pointed at her.

'I'm gonna set something up for us. I got you, gummy bear.'

He took one last glance at Marcus' painting, booped Ginny on the nose and meandered out of her room. He paused at the threshold, one hand on the door frame.

'You should come hang out with the rest of us if you can. It'd be good to sit together as a family.'

Ginny gazed back as he smiled warmly at her. How she longed to bask in her father's presence. He tapped the door frame twice with his palm and made his exit.

Ginny exhaled slowly and turned back to her computer.

As a family.

She wasn't sure the Miller household knew the meaning anymore.

o

o - o

o - o - o

o - o

o

Ginny was woken by movement in her bed. Half-asleep, she turned and saw Georgia climbing into bed next to her, face drawn and quiet.

Ginny sighed and stared u Georgia settled in on her side and looked at Ginny.

'I'm sleeping with you tonight,' Georgia whispered.

Ginny widened her eyes and raised her eyebrows excessively, feigning surprise.

'Grump,' muttered Georgia, and she sighed.

Silence draped over them heavily, weighted down with all the words they hadn't said to each other over the last number of days. Georgia was so close Ginny could of her mother's body, but a deep chasm had been gouged out between them, and Ginny was almost fascinated to find how far, far away she could feel. There was a anchor tied around her feet as it pulled her inexorably further away, but nevertheless there was a tiny twine of nearly-abandoned hope that Ginny desperately clung After many tense moments Georgia reached out a gentle hand and brushed Ginny's cheek. Ginny blinked at the tenderness, a small lump forming in her throat.

'I hate when we fight, peach.'

Ginny's heart thumped painfully, and she waited with baited breath. Her mind ran amok with the sound of Georgia's hand smacking across her face, the resulting st glisten of unshed tears in Georgia's eyes after a call to the local police enforcement, the sunken skin under them the next day. Ginny suddenly burned with the urge fallout of her friends, but she pinched her lips together.

Georgia took a big inhale.

'Ginny, I...I'm sorry. I never meant to hurt you.'

Ginny swallowed, her ears almost ringing with the sheer focus she now sent to her auditory sense.

'But you did,' she whispered.

These were the first words she'd spoken to her mother in days.

'I know. I was angry. I shouldn't...' Georgia's voice trembled slightly. She cleared her throat. 'I won't apologise for being angry,' she added sternly. 'You snuck out, I you to own up to that much.'

'I did sneak out.'

'But I...I was wrong to do...what I did.'

Ginny finally looked over at her mom and was surprised to see tear tracks down Georgia's face.

'Everything I do is for you, and for Austin. I want you to have everything I never had,' she continued in a thick voice. 'And I was too angry to see...'

Ginny's eyes grew uncomfortable and her vision swam. She had never seen her mother like this, never heard her mother speak like this.

'If that had gone wrong...' Georgia stopped, as if unable to speak about what might have happened if Ginny had been in the Baker house when the police arrived. S

shuddering breath. 'I love you, peach, and I'm sorry I ever might have made you question that.'

Hot tears leaked across Ginny's face as she stared at her mother. This beautiful, strong and proud woman. Never, even after a breakup with her father, never had s humility and sorrow touch her face.

Georgia leaned forward and kissed Ginny firmly on her forehead. Ginny allowed her touch; it was so familiar but it felt alien too. Nevertheless, Ginny found that she pulling herself along that little hope-twine that she knew would carry her back. She tucked herself against her mother's chest, coming to rest under her chin. The d grief inside her – filled with her doubts and insecurities, the colour of her skin and how the world reflected back at her because of it, the questions burned into her lifestyle, the strength of a mother's hand, and the vengeance that Georgia had shown herself capable – it rose up, and up, as Georgia wrapped an arm around Ginn Ginny's eyes and throat; she shuddered as thick sobs fell from her hard and unending.

And as Georgia's hand soothed her back, Ginny was little and malleable, putty in the hands of Georgia, with pudgy arms and tiny fingers with no core strength to h She was recently mobile and bouncing on her mom's knee, she was tearing through the house with outstretched arms and cries of glee as fast as her wobbly legs w while Georgia followed. She was curled up with her thumb in her mouth while resting on Georgia's chest, with Georgia murmuring quiet nonsense in her little toddle rustle of her curly hair pleasantly familiar. She was safe.

It had been so long.

Georgia gently stroked Ginny's hair, tears in her own eyes.

'Shh, baby girl.'

Ginny let Georgia coax her into relaxation, and her sobs gradually minimised. Georgia began to pat Ginny's back.

'I'm not that much of a baby,' Ginny whispered with a thick voice, but the corners of her mouth were upturned.

'Hush, you're my little baby.' Georgia closed her eyes resolutely and shook her head to dash away Ginny's words.

'I'm sixteen,' Ginny reminded her, sniffing and wiping her wet cheek.

'Okay, you can be my big baby.' She kissed the top of Ginny's hair, allowing her face to nuzzle in it. 'But you will always be my baby.'

Ginny closed her eyes and sank further into Georgia's arms until the wetness of her face grew uncomfortable. She removed herself from their hug and grabbed a tis bedside table, dabbing at her moist skin. She blew her nose not so elegantly.

'Gross,' Georgia said lightly.

'You are,' Ginny shot back immaturely, disposing of her tissue. But she grinned and slid back down comfortably next to Georgia.

Ginny glanced over at Georgia, who had recently wiped her own tears away.

'...you can't sleep?' she asked.

'Mm-mm.'

'Dad's back...'

'Oh, is he? I hadn't noticed.'

Ginny rolled over to face Georgia.

'Mom, just...' she said gently, 'Just...please don't do anything stupid.'

213

Georgia frowned.

'What do you mean?'

'...I've never seen you this happy. This job, this town. Paul,' Ginny added with mild disdain.

Georgia smiled.

'And you and I both know that you're in bed with me so that you don't go to Dad,' Ginny continued.

'We don't know that,' Georgia said a little too seriously.

'...Can he just be my dad this time? Instead of your ex?'

'You have nothing to worry about with your dad and me, peach. I promise, okay?'

Ginny stared at Georgia and felt the warmth in her chest ebb away. Those eyes she'd known her whole life gazed with sincerity at Ginny while she told a blatant lie, reminding her that absolutely anything that came out of Mary's mouth could not be trusted.

She could count on her mom loving her. But she couldn't count on anything else.

o

o - o

o - o - o

o - o

o

Ginny was so happy she was practically vibrating as she put her phone – newly on silent at Zion's request – in her pocket, but she played it cool as they walked into dimly lit bar with lots of cosy seats and twinkle lights, buzzing with the quiet conversation of its patrons.

'So, what do you think?' he asked.

'Um, I don't know. Whatever.' Ginny looked around with the bare minimum level of interest.

She wasn't sure what they were doing here. "You'll love it," Zion had told her mysteriously as she'd climbed on the bike behind him.

'Oh! Okay, I see. So, you're - you're cool now.' Zion teased, leading her deeper inside.

'No, I'm not. Cool people don't say they're cool.'

'Hmm, taking notes. Must be cool.'

They sat in an almost overstuffed leather chair close to the front of a stage. Ginny wondered if it was an open-mic night, but there was only one microphone on sta instruments. Did her dad bring her to a lecture?

As she got comfortable, Zion reached an arm out and pulled her over to him playfully. Ginny's face lit up like fireworks and she giggled as she only ever did with him smell of her dad filled her senses – well-worn leather and soap. The most comforting smell in the world.

She rested in the crook of his elbow along the back of the chair, perfectly at home, and slightly eager for what awaited them on stage.

215

'So what else is going on?' Zion asked, smiling warmly.

Ginny looked towards the ceiling as she pondered what she would say.

'Hmm. Mom's a psychopath.'

'Hey!'

'Did you know she has a sister?' Ginny pulled away from her dad so she could look at him more squarely.

'Ah, you met Maddie?'

'Did you know her parents are still alive? So apparently I have grandparents that I never knew about. That's not fair – to keep a kid from their grandparents.'

'Look, I get it. I know. But I met your grandparents, and...to Georgia, they are dead. She did what she did so she could be the best mom she could be. Your mom I than anything. And so do I.'

Ginny hated the soft and adoring tone that Zion used when he spoke about Georgia.

'Okay, fine. But she is crazy.'

'Come on.'

'You're seriously gonna tell me that she's not crazy?'

'Alright, I'm not gonna say that. Yeah, your mom's mad cray. But she's the kind of crazy that you want on your side.'

Before Ginny could retort, the sound of gentle clicking from the bar patrons interrupted their conversation as a man took to the stage their chair faced. Ginny joined heartedly with one hand, looking around in confusion.

The man took a breath and started.

' If home is where the heart is

then as a traveler

my home is nomadic. '

And Ginny was hooked.

In her pocket, unknown to Ginny, her phone lit up many times over the course of the next two and a half hours. She was enraptured in the souls being bared on sta and the rhythm of words that danced, and her father's own piece to her. She never once checked her phone.

8:17pm

M: Hey, can I come over?

Or would you wanna come here?

8:56pm

M: You there?

9:29pm

M: Are you okay?

9:46pm

M: Is everything alright with your mom?

Let me know if you need me.

9:47pm

M: This double texting is embarrassing.

9:55pm

M: Imma break the rule just this once

and check on you. [window emoji]

You can kill me later.

10:02pm

M: ...so I messed up.

your mom saw me

Printed in Great Britain
by Amazon

31317306R00126